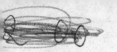

KU-166-361

Enid Blyton's

A BOOK OF
ANIMAL STORIES

First published 1989

Published by Dean, an imprint of
The Hamlyn Publishing Group Limited
Michelin House, 81 Fulham Road,
London SW3 6RB, England.

Text copyright © Darrell Waters Limited 1950,
1951, 1952, 1953, 1954, 1955

Illustrations copyright
© The Hamlyn Publishing Group Limited 1989

ISBN 0 600 56326 X

All rights reserved. No part of this publication
may be reproduced, stored in a retrieval system,
or transmitted in any form or by any means,
electronic, mechanical, photocopying, recording
or otherwise, without the permission of
The Hamlyn Publishing Group Limited
and the copyright holders.

Printed in Great Britain
at The Bath Press, Avon

Enid Blyton's
A BOOK OF
ANIMAL STORIES

DEAN

THE ENID BLYTON TRUST
FOR CHILDREN

We hope you will enjoy this book. Please think for
a moment about those children who are too ill to
do the exciting things you and your friends do.

Help them by sending a donation, large or
small, to THE ENID BLYTON TRUST FOR CHILDREN.
The Trust will use all your gifts to help
children who are sick or handicapped and need
to be made happy and comfortable.

Please send your postal order or cheque to:
The Enid Blyton Trust for Children,
3rd Floor, New South Wales House,
15 Adam Street, Strand,
London WC2N 6AH

Thank you very much for your help.

CONTENTS

The Cat that was Forgotten

ONCE there was a big black cat called Sootikin. He lived with the Jones family, and he killed all the mice that came to eat their crumbs.

Sootikin was a fine cat. His eyes were as green as cucumbers, and his whiskers were as white as snow. He was always purring, and he loved to be petted.

But the Jones family didn't pet him very much. Hilda and Ronnie Jones were not very fond of animals, and Mrs. Jones often shouted at him because he mewed round her feet when she was cooking fish.

Next door lived a boy called Billy. He loved Sootikin. He thought he was the finest cat in the world, and he was always looking out for him to stroke him.

"I wish Sootikin was mine, Mummy," he said to his mother. "I wish we had a cat."

But his mother didn't like cats or dogs in the house, though she often said she liked Sootikin, and wished he would come and kill the mice in her larder.

Now one day the Jones family were very

excited. They called over the fence to Billy.

"We're going away for a whole month to the seaside, to our Granny's. Aren't we lucky?"

"Yes," said Billy, who had never even seen the sea. "How I wish I was going with you!"

"We're catching the ten o'clock train," said Hilda. "We'll send you a postcard."

All the Jones family got into a taxi-cab at half-past nine and went off to the station. Billy felt lonely. He liked hearing the children next door shouting and laughing. Now for a whole month their house would be empty.

"I suppose they've taken dear old Sootikin too," he thought.

But they hadn't, because, to Billy's great surprise, the big black cat suddenly sprang on to the top of the wall, and curled himself up in the sun. "Mummy. The Joneses haven't taken Sootikin," said Billy. "Isn't that funny?"

"Oh, I expect they have arranged with a friend of theirs to come and feed him every day," said Mummy. "That is what people usually do when they have animals they leave behind. Maybe someone will come along with bread and milk or a bit of fish each day."

Sootikin wondered where his family had gone. They hadn't even said good-bye to him. He went to the kitchen door after a bit and mewed to get in. But nobody opened the door. He went to see if he could find an open window, but they were all shut.

All that day Sootikin felt lonely, but he felt sure his family would come back in the evening. Then he could go indoors, have his milk, and jump into his own basket.

But his family didn't come back. Sootikin began to feel very hungry. There were no mice to catch, because he had caught them all. He wished he could have something to eat.

He had to sleep outside that night because he couldn't get into his house. It rained, and although Sootikin was under a bush, he got very wet. He sneezed.

He felt sad. His family had gone. They had forgotten him. They hadn't left him any food. They hadn't remembered that he had nowhere to sleep. They didn't love him at all. They were unkind.

He was very hungry the next day and the next. He found an old kipper bone and ate that. He chewed up an old crust.

When the fourth day came, he was thin and his coat looked rough and untidy. He had a cold. He didn't feel at all well, but he still felt hungry.

He thought of Billy, the boy next door. He had always been kind to him. Perhaps he would give him something to eat.

So Sootikin jumped over the wall to find Billy. He was in the garden, digging. Sootikin mewed.

Billy turned round. At first he hardly knew Sootikin, for the poor cat was so thin and his coat was no longer silky and smooth.

"Why – is it *you*, Sootikin!" cried Billy, and he bent down to stroke the cat. "Poor, poor thing – you look so thin and hungry. Has no one been feeding you?"

Sootikin mewed to say that no one had fed him, he was lonely and sad, and please could he have something to eat.

Billy understood, and ran to his mother. "Mummy," he cried, "poor old Sootikin is half-starved. Look at him – all skin and bone. Oh, Mummy, can I give him something to eat?"

"Poor creature!" said his mother, putting down a plate of fish scraps and milk. "Here you are, Sootikin. He's got a cold too, Billy – he must have slept out in the rain at night."

"Mummy, could he sleep in our kitchen till his cold is better?" said Billy. His mother nodded. She was kind and she didn't like to think that Sootikin had been forgotten like that.

Sootikin was glad. He ate a good meal and felt better. He washed himself and made his fur silkier. Then he jumped into a box that Billy had found for him, and went fast asleep.

He slept all night in the kitchen. He had a good meal the next day, and he slept the next night in the kitchen too – but not *all* night! No – he heard the mice in the larder, and he went to see what they were up to. Sootikin knew that mice were not allowed in larders.

Sootikin killed three big mice and one little one. He left them in a row to show Billy's mother what he had done. She was very pleased when she saw the mice.

"Mummy, that's Sootikin's way of saying thank you for our kindness," said Billy, stroking the big cat, who purred loudly. "Oh, Mummy, I do love Sootikin. I do wish he was my cat."

"Well, the Joneses will want him as soon as they come back," said his mother. "You must make the most of him whilst they are away. I do think it was unkind of them to forget all about him like this."

But do you know, when the Jones family came back, Sootikin wouldn't live with them any more. He simply wouldn't. Every time Billy put him over the wall, he came back again.

"He just won't live with us," said Hilda. "Silly cat. He doesn't know his own home."

"Well – you didn't seem to know your own cat – you forgot all about him," said Billy. "You don't deserve a cat like Sootikin. I hope he *does* live with us, and not you!"

Sootikin did. He had quite made up his mind about that. He never went into the Joneses' garden or house again but kept close to Billy.

"A cat can't help loving people who are kind," purred Sootikin. "I'm *your* cat now, Billy, and you're my little boy!"

The Frisky Little Goat

IT HAD been raining very hard, but now the sun looked as if it was just coming out.

Jack stood at the window and wished he could go out. He wanted to see if there were any blackberries ripe. He felt as if he could eat about a hundred nice juicy ones.

"Mummy, can I go out?" he called.

"No," said Mummy. "It's too wet. There are great big puddles everywhere, and the grass is soaking."

"I do want to go out," said Jack. "I want to see if there are any blackberries."

"You heard what I said," said Mummy. So Jack didn't say any more. He went on looking out of the window, wishing and wishing that he was out with the ducks. They liked the wet. They splashed through all the puddles and had a lovely time.

Someone came to see his mother. They went into the drawing-room and shut the door. Jack stayed still, thinking hard.

He could slip out whilst his mother was

talking. It was Mrs. Jones who had come, and she always stayed a very long time. He could go to the field where the blackberries grew, pick some, and then slip back before his mother knew. It would be fun, he thought, to run in and out without anyone knowing.

Jack was not a very obedient little boy. He often disobeyed his mother, and she got very cross with him. He knew he ought not to disobey now – but he did so badly want those blackberries.

"I won't go into any puddles. I'll try not to get into the long wet grass," he thought. "Then I shan't get my feet wet."

He slipped out of the garden door. He went across the garden, taking care not to tread in any puddles. He only had on his brown sandals, so he had to be very careful indeed.

He came to the field and climbed over the gate. Then down he jumped and made his way to the hedge where the blackberries grew.

He didn't see a frisky little nanny-goat in the field. But the nanny-goat saw him. Ha, a little boy to play with! That was nice.

The goat trotted up to Jack and bleated. It made him jump. He turned round and saw the goat. He was afraid of goats.

"Go away," he said, but the goat didn't go away. It stood there bleating. Then it skipped high in the air, put down its head and butted Jack lightly on the legs.

"Don't!" said Jack, in fright, and tried to run away. But the goat thought the little boy was playing a game with it, and it was full of joy and liveliness.

It ran playfully at Jack, and he screamed. He ran as fast as his legs would take him, and the goat skipped behind him, butting him every now and again.

Jack splashed through enormous puddles. He stumbled over muddy patches and splashed his legs with mud up to the knees. He cried big tears all down his cheeks.

The goat wouldn't let him get over the gate. It frisked round him, and every time he tried to climb up, the goat butted him down.

Jack saw a gap in the hedge and ran for that. But the goat was there first. Jack ran another way, and the goat ran after him, enjoying the game very much. It thought the little boy was a fine play-mate.

The goat butted Jack a bit harder, and he fell into an enormous puddle. He was soaked from head to foot! Whatever would his mother say!

Somehow he managed to scramble through the gap. But, of course, the goat went through after him too! So there was Jack, racing for his house, and the goat skipping and tripping all round him!

Jack rushed in through the door, and the goat rushed in too. His mother was just coming into the hall, holding Jack's wellington boots in her hand.

She stared in great surprise at Jack and the goat. "Whatever are you and the goat doing?" she said, and she shooed the goat out of the door. It went back to its field, pleased to have had such a fine game.

"Jack! Where have you been? Whatever have you been doing to yourself?" said his mother. "Look at your sandals soaked through – and your socks – and all your clothes muddy and torn. What have you been doing?"

"I went to get some blackberries," wept Jack.

"Then you are a naughty, disobedient little boy," said Mummy, crossly. "I told you it was too wet. Now see what has happened to you!"

"The goat chased me," sobbed Jack. "It chased me home!"

"It wouldn't have chased you if you hadn't disobeyed me and gone out," said Mummy. "And see – I had just gone to get your wellington boots for you, and I was going to tell you to put them on, and go and find some blackberries! If you had obeyed me, you would still have been indoors, and could have put on your boots and gone out."

"The goat would still have chased me," said Jack.

"No, it wouldn't," said Mummy, "because I should have told you not to go into that field. It is only a playful little thing, anyway – it couldn't do you much harm if you were sensible and didn't run away and fall over."

"I'm sorry, Mummy," said Jack.

"So am I," said Mummy. "Sorrier than you because now that you have spoilt your clothes, you can't go out to tea this afternoon. Your other jumpers are being washed – this is the only one you have clean, and now it is wet and dirty and torn."

"I didn't know I was to go out to tea," said Jack.

"Well, Mrs. Jones came to ask if you could go to a party with her little grandson," said Mummy. "Now you won't be able to go. Well – you shouldn't have been disobedient. Until you learn to be sensible and obey, you will find things often go wrong. You had better go upstairs now and get washed!"

Jack was silly, wasn't he? If he hadn't disobeyed, he could have put on his wellington boots, played with the goat instead of running away, and had a lovely time at the party. Perhaps he will be more sensible another time!

Good Old Miner the Mole!

ONCE upon a time there was great excitement in Rabbit-Town. All the bunnies met together and talked for a long time.

"The green goblins have said they are going to come here, to our burrows, catch us, and keep us for servants," said Floppy, the chief rabbit.

"How wicked!" cried everyone.

"They are small creatures and can easily get down our burrows," said Bobtail. "They have only got to put a guard at each entrance, and send goblins down into our holes, to be able to catch all of us easily!"

"If we can't get out of our front doors or our back doors, we can't help being caught," said Whiskers.

"Well, what are we going to do, then?" said Floppy.

"How are the goblins going to get here?" asked Whiskers. "They live the other side of the river. They can't swim, and I know they have no boats."

"They have little aeroplanes," said Bobtail.

"They got the wizard Tall-Hat to make them for them. They can fly them easily. The aeroplanes have wheels underneath, just as real ones have, and they will easily land on our smooth hillside."

All the rabbits stared at one another in fear. Whatever could they do to stop the goblins?

"It's a pity the hillside is so smooth and grassy," said Floppy.

"Well, we have made it like that by nibbling the grass every evening," said Bobtail. "If only we could make the hillside bumpy, so that aeroplanes can't land!"

A little rabbit who was listening came shyly up. "Please," he said, "I think I know someone who could help you. He could make the hillside full of bumps and lumps!"

"What do you mean, Furry?" said Floppy in surprise. "Make the hillside full of bumps and lumps! Who is this that can do such a thing?"

"It's a friend of mine, Miner the mole," said Furry, his nose trembling because he was so shy. "He throws up little hills wherever he goes, because he makes tunnels, you see – and if I asked him to tunnel under the grass on our hillside he could make so many hills that the goblin aeroplanes couldn't land!"

"Well, well, what an idea!" said Bobtail. "Fetch this friend of yours here."

Furry sped away down the burrow. He went to a burrow a good way away and listened. He could hear someone scratching and digging not far off. He drummed with his hind paws on the ground.

"Miner the mole! Miner the mole! It is your friend Furry calling you! I want you! Dig this way."

Miner the mole, who had very sharp hearing indeed, tunnelled his way towards the burrow where Furry sat. Soon he broke through the wall, and his little snout looked through.

"Miner the mole! Come with me!" said Furry. "I will tell you everything as we go along. I believe you can save us rabbits from the green goblins!"

He told the mole everything as they went along the burrows, back to the rabbits' meeting. The big rabbits stared at the curious little mole.

"Is this Miner the mole?" said Floppy. "Good-day to you, mole. I hear that you spend your time tunnelling through the earth, and throwing up little hills as you go."

"Well, I've got to put the earth somewhere,"

said the mole. He was much smaller than the rabbits, and his fur looked very velvety. It did not grow all one way as the fur of the rabbits did – it could be stroked either forwards or backwards.

"Why do you burrow and tunnel so much?" asked Bobtail. "You don't live in your burrow as we do, do you?"

"Oh no," said the mole. "I tunnel because I want food. You see, I am always hungry, and I have to hunt for my food. It's easy to get food if you eat the grass that grows on the hillside. But I don't like grass."

"What do you like to eat, then?" asked

Whiskers. " We love eating grass."

"Oh, beetles, and worms and all kinds of grubs I find under the ground," said Miner the mole. "I dig after them, you see, and I eat hundreds. Look at my front paws – they are specially made for digging."

He held them out. They were strange paws, turned outwards for digging. "They are like spades!" said Whiskers. "What strong claws you have! You are a real little miner, mole!"

"What do you want me to do for you?" asked the mole. "Tell me, please, because I feel hungry again and I want to get back to my digging. I could do with a few beetles and slugs for my dinner."

"Well, I am sure you will find plenty under the grass on our hillside," said Floppy. "We will take you and show you where to dig – and we do beg of you, mole, to throw up as many hills as you can, so that when the goblins come to land their aeroplanes, they will all crash!"

The rabbits took the mole out to the hillside. "Right!" said Miner the mole. "I'll begin just here – and I'll throw up line after line of molehills, so look out!"

The rabbits watched him – and even as they looked, the mole seemed to sink into the ground! His enormously strong front paws worked like powerful spades, and he dug a hole for himself so fast that it seemed as if he sank into the ground. In half a minute he was gone!

And then the rabbits saw molehills rising one by one down the smooth hillside! It was strange to see them! As the mole tunnelled , he threw up the earth that he scraped away, and it rose in little hillocks behind him.

"What did I tell you!" cried Furry in delight. "Didn't I say he would cover the hillside with bumps and lumps? Wasn't I right? Just look at all the little mounds he is making!"

Miner the mole worked in a long line, and behind him rose a row of hillocks of earth. Then he turned, went to the right, and began to tunnel back again, up the hill, instead of down. And behind him rose the lumps and bumps of earth again.

"Oh, it's wonderful to watch Miner the mole at work," said Whiskers. "Really wonderful! What a fine tunneller he is! Why, the whole countryside must be tunnelled by the moles, hunting for their food all the time!"

Soon the hillside was covered with mounds. There were dozens of them. The rabbits were delighted.

"What a shock for the green goblins when they try to land in their aeroplanes!" they cried. "What a surprise for them!"

It was indeed! Two days later, in the early morning, the green goblins set off to catch the rabbits for their servants. They got into their neat little aeroplanes, set the engines going, and rose into the air. The rabbits across the river heard the roar of the small engines.

"Here they come!" they cried, and every rabbit ran to the entrance of his burrow to watch what would happen.

"R-r-r-r-r-r-r!" The aeroplanes came skimming over the river to the hillside. The green goblins looked for a good place to land.

But what was this? There was nowhere to land! The hillside was covered with lumps and bumps of earth!

"We can't land in safety!" shouted the goblins to one another. "The mole has been at work! He has covered the hillside with mounds of earth. We shall crash if we try to land."

They tried to find landing-places farther down the hill, but they couldn't, for there were so many bushes there. So they had to fly back again across the river, and leave the rabbits in peace.

"Hurray!" cried all the rabbits, coming out and frisking round. "Hurray! The green goblins have gone. We are safe! Miner the mole, come up and let us tell you how you have saved us!"

Miner the mole poked his little snout up and grinned at the excited rabbits.

"Don't bother to thank me," he said. "I have had such a good feast! There were hundreds of beetles and grubs in your hillside. I shall get as fat as butter soon! Good-bye!"

He disappeared into the earth, and the rabbits saw another line of hillocks growing, as he tunnelled quickly down the hillside.

"Good old Miner the mole!" they said. "Furry, it was a fine idea of yours to get him!" You shall have the very best burrow to live in, all to yourself!"

The green goblins never came back again, so the rabbits were safe. They flew away in their little aeroplanes and nobody has ever heard of them since.

We Are Your Friends

TOMMY was a little town boy. He raced about the streets, shouted and yelled, chased all the cats he saw, and shooed away the pigeons. He was that sort of boy.

Then one day he went to stay with his uncle in the country. Uncle George had a farm. He kept cows, sheep, hens, and geese, so it was an exciting place to stay at. He had dogs and cats as well.

Tommy had never seen so many animals and birds in his life. He shouted at them to make them run away. He threw stones to frighten them. He chased them.

The dogs would have bitten him if he hadn't been such a small boy. The cats would have scratched him if they had got near enough. None of the creatures liked Tommy.

"Why is he so cruel to us?" they said to one another. "We are his friends! What a funny boy to chase us away and shout and throw stones! Doesn't he *know* that we are his friends?"

27

"Shall we treat him in the same way?" said a cow with big horns. "I could toss him easily."

"And I could chase him, and hiss at him and peck him," said the biggest goose.

"And I wouldn't mind nipping his leg if it would teach him a lesson," said one of the dogs.

"Well," said a sheep, "if we did that, it would make him think we were his enemies, not his friends. He would hate us all the more – and hatred is a horrid thing, cruel and cold."

"It would be better to teach him to love us," said another cow, mooing softly. "You see –Tommy is really more foolish than bad. He doesn't know we are his friends!"

"Well, we will all tell him, then," said the biggest dog. "See, there he is in the corner of the field. He has fallen asleep in the sun. Let's go and talk to him."

So they all went to where Tommy lay fast asleep. They stood round him in a circle, the big cows outside, the sheep next, the dogs next, the geese next, then the hens and the cats. The biggest cow mooed to wake Tommy.

He opened his eyes and sat up. When he saw all the birds and animals round him, he was very frightened.

"Go away," he said. "Have you come to bite me and scratch me and poke me with your horns? Go away! I don't like you, and I'm sure you don't like *me*."

"Tommy, we are your friends," mooed the big cow. "We have come to tell you."

"Don't be silly," said Tommy. "How can you be my friends? You don't do anything for me! You just run about the fields and eat."

"We do a lot of things for you," said the cow. "Why, you could hardly live without us! We give you so very many presents."

"I don't believe you," said Tommy.

"Now listen," said the cow. "I give you milk each day, and cream. I give you butter for your bread. I give you cheese as well. Don't you think those are lovely presents?"

"And I give you the wool for your warm jerseys and your socks," said the sheep. "The vest you wear is made of my wool too. I keep you warm."

"And I guard your house," said the biggest dog. "I keep foxes away from the chickens. I find any sheep that are lost. I am your guardian, and the sheep's too."

"And I give you the feathers in your pillow," said the biggest goose. "Isn't your pillow soft and warm at night? Well, your aunt filled it with my feathers. That is my present to you."

"And we catch all the mice and rats that steal your food," said a big tabby cat. "We work very hard each night. We live round the barns, and we are always watching for your enemies, the mice and the rats."

"And we lay eggs for your breakfast and your tea," said a brown hen in a loud, clucking voice. "Isn't that a friendly thing to do? Why should you throw stones at us, Tommy, when we lay eggs for you to eat?"

Tommy looked so surprised. "Do you all do so much for me?" he said, and he felt ashamed. "Are you really my friends?"

"Well, isn't it a friendly thing to do, to give you so many presents, and to work so hard for you and your family?" said the big dog. "All we ask in return is a little food and shelter – and some friendliness too. We all like a kind word, or a pat. I know *I* do!"

"I've been silly," said Tommy, getting up. "I didn't know you were my friends. Please, I didn't *know*. I'm not a cruel little boy really. I just didn't *know*!"

"Well, couldn't you think a bit and find out before you treat creatures badly?" said the big cow. "You could listen to what people say, you could read books, you could be wise instead of foolish – and wise people are never cruel. It is only stupid people, or wicked ones who are cruel."

"I'm not wicked – I've been stupid and that has made me do things a cruel person would do," said Tommy. "I want to be friends with you now, if you'll let me. I didn't know you did all those things for me."

"It's a good rule always to be friendly," said a dog. "We are – until we know someone is really an enemy. Then we bite. But we are friendly first."

"I'll be friendly too," said Tommy. "I'll come and talk to you each day, and I'll never shout at you, or throw stones. Thank you for telling me everything. I'm glad you are my friends. I want to be yours too."

So Tommy is friends with all the animals and birds now, and he is much happier than before. Wasn't it nice of them to go and tell him they were his friends? They are yours too, of course.

The Silly Little Cat

TIPTOE was a pretty little cat, and she knew it. She was black with a white front and four white paws, and could jump and climb marvellously.

She was very vain. "I'm the prettiest cat in the road!" she told the others. "And I can jump the highest too. See me leap right up to the top of the wall!"

And up she leapt in one bound. She certainly was very clever indeed. But nobody likes clever people if they keep talking about themselves, and the other cats turned their backs on Tiptoe whenever she came by.

"Last night I caught six mice," Tiptoe told them. "My mistress says she has never had such a good mouser as I am."

Old Tom, the slyest cat there, swished his long black tail and looked at Tiptoe.

"Ah, clever you may be, Tiptoe," he said, "but there's something you can't do! I once saw a cat do it, so it can be done, but I am *sure* you couldn't do it!"

"Well, if a cat has done it, *I* can do it," said Tiptoe at once. "Tell me."

"Do you see that tall flagpost that goes almost up to the sky?" said old Tom. "Well, I once saw a cat go up to the top. What a climb! You couldn't do that, Tiptoe!"

"Oh yes I could!" said Tiptoe, and she ran to the flagpost. "I can climb anything!"

Tabby jumped up to stop her. "Tiptoe! Don't be silly! You will never get down again."

"Let her go," said old Tom slyly. "It will keep her out of our way for a long, long time. She'll have to stay there for ages. She won't talk about climbing again, *or* how clever she is!"

Tiptoe climbed up the flagpost. What a long way it was to the top! She panted and puffed, but up she went, digging her claws into the wood. And at last there she was, on the very top, balancing herself on the round knob.

She was just opening her mouth to mew to the others to see how clever she was, when she saw how far she was from the ground. Goodness! Could that be the ground, so far away? And were those little specks the other cats, watching her? Tiptoe was terrified.

She wobbled a bit. She dug her claws in hard. She would never, never be able to get down. She would fall if she even looked down again. Oh, what was she to do?

"I've been so stupid!" she wailed to herself. "I wanted to show off, and now see where I've put myself! Somewhere terrible. I shall have to stay here all my life long."

Well, she stayed there for two hours, feeling more and more frightened. Presently a boy came along and saw her. He was most upset.

"Poor little cat," he thought, "I must tell the policeman so that he can rescue her."

The policeman said he couldn't, of course. But he went to the fire station and got the firemen to bring the fire-escape out. They took it to the flagpost – but Tiptoe wouldn't jump on it. She was much too frightened. So a fireman went up, lifted her off the flagpost, put her on his shoulder, and brought her down.

"Well, perhaps that will teach Tiptoe not to think she's so clever, and stop her boasting any more!" said old Tom. "We shall have some peace at last!"

The next morning Tiptoe walked up to her friends proudly. "I'm the cat they told the policeman about!" she said. "I'm the cat they brought the fire-escape for! I really am the most remarkable cat in the world!"

Well, well, what do you think of *that*? You just can't teach some people anything, can you?

The Cross Little Tadpole

ONCE upon a time a big mass of jelly lay on the top of a pond. In it were tiny black specks, like little black commas.

The sun shone down and warmed the jelly. A fish tried to nibble a bit, but it was too slippery. A big black beetle tried a little too, but he didn't like it. The rain came and pattered down on the jelly.

Every day the tiny black specks grew bigger. They were eggs. Soon it would be time for them to hatch, and swim about as tadpoles in the pond.

The day came when the black eggs had become wriggling tadpoles, and then the jelly began to disappear. It was no longer needed. It had saved the eggs from being eaten, because it was too slippery for any creature to gobble up for its dinner. It had helped to hold the eggs up to the sunshine too. But now it was of no more use.

The little black wrigglers swam to a water-weed and held on to it. They were very tiny.

When they were hungry they nibbled the weed.
It tasted nice to them.

They grew bigger each day in the pond, and
soon the other creatures began to know them.
"There go two tadpoles!" said the stickleback,
all his spines standing up along his back.

"Funny creatures, aren't they?" said the big
black beetle. "All head and tail – nothing much
else to them!"

"Hundreds of them!" said the water-snail.
"The whole pond is full of them."

"I like them for my dinner," said the
dragonfly grub. "Look – I hide down here in
the mud, and when I see a nice fat tadpole
swimming by, out I pounce and catch one in
my jaw."

A good many of the tadpoles were eaten by
enemies, because they were not clever enough
or fast enough to escape. Those that were left
grew big, and raced about the pond, wriggling
their long tails swiftly.

One little tadpole had some narrow escapes.
One of the black beetles nearly caught him – in
fact, a tiny piece was bitten off his tail. Another
time he scraped himself badly on the spines of
the stickleback. And twice the dragonfly grub
darted at him and almost caught him. Each time

the little tadpole was very cross.

"Leave me alone! What harm am I doing to you? I don't want to be your dinner!"

The pond had other things in it besides the fish, the grubs, and the beetles. It had some frogs, and the little tadpole was always in a temper about these.

"Those big fat frogs are so rude and bad-mannered," he said to the other tadpoles. "How I hate them with their gaping mouths and great big eyes!"

The frogs didn't like the cross little tadpole

37

because he called rude names after them. Sometimes they chased him, swimming fast with their strong hind legs.

"If we catch you, we shall spank you hard!" they croaked. The tadpole swam behind a stone and called back to them, "Old croakers! Old greedy-mouths! Old stick-out eyes!"

The frogs tried to overturn the stone and get at the rude tadpole. But he burrowed down in the mud, and came up far behind them.

"Old croakers!" he cried. "Here I am –peep-bo! Old croakers!"

The frogs lay in wait for the rude tadpole. He never knew when a fat green frog would jump into the water from the bank, almost on top of him. He never knew when one would scramble out of the mud just below him.

"I'm tired of these frogs," he told the other tadpoles. "I wish somebody would eat them. I wish those ducks would come back and gobble them up!"

The tadpole had never forgotten one day when some wild ducks had flown down to the pond, and had frightened all the frogs and other creatures very much indeed.

The ducks had caught and eaten three frogs, and at least twenty tadpoles. It had been a dreadful day. None of the tadpoles ever forgot it.

"You shouldn't wish for those ducks to come back!" said the stickleback. "*You* might be eaten yourself!"

"I'm getting too big to be eaten," said the cross tadpole. "Stickleback, what else eats frogs?"

"The grass-snake eats frogs," said the pretty little stickleback. "I once saw him come sliding down into the water. He swam beautifully. He ate four frogs when he came."

"I've a good mind to go and tell him to come to this pond and eat some more frogs," said the tadpole. "He might be glad to know there was a good meal here for him."

"Well, he is lying in the sun on the bank of the pond over there," said the stickleback. "Go and tell him now! But, tadpole – listen to me – I don't think I have ever met anyone quite so silly as you in all my life!"

"Pooh!" said the tadpole rudely, and swam off towards the bank on which the long grass-snake was lying, curled up in a heap.

The tadpole poked his black head out of the water and called to the snake, "Hi, grass-snake! Can you hear me?"

The snake woke up in surprise. He looked at the tadpole. "What do you want?" he said.

"I've come to tell you that there are a lot of horrid, nasty frogs in this pond, that would make a very good dinner for you," said the tadpole. "If you slide into the water now I'll show you where to look for them. I'd be glad if you would eat every frog you can see, because they lie in wait for me and try to catch me and spank me."

The snake put out his quivering tongue and then drew it in again. "I would come today, but I have just had a very good meal," he said. "I will come back some day when I am hungry, and you shall show me where to find the frogs then."

He glided off through the grass. The tadpole swam back to his friends in excitement.

"What do you think?" he cried. "I've told the grass-snake about those horrid frogs that want to spank me! He is coming back to eat them one day soon!"

The days went on, warm, sunny days. The tadpole grew and grew. One day he noticed that he had two back legs, and he was most astonished.

"Hallo!" he said. "I've got legs! So have all

the other tadpoles. Rather nice!"

Then he noticed that he had front legs as well. His tail became shorter. He wanted to breathe up in the air, instead of breathing down in the water.

He and the other tadpoles found a little bit of wood on the surface of the water, and they climbed up on to it. It was nice to sit there in the sunshine, breathing the warm air. It was fun to flick out a little tongue to see if any fly could be caught by it.

"This is a nice life!" said the cross tadpole. "A very nice life. I like living in this warm pond. Most of those horrid frogs have gone now, so life is very pleasant."

"There's your friend, the grass-snake," said the stickleback, poking his head up suddenly. "Why don't you go and tell him to come and gobble up all the frogs in this pond, as you said you would?"

The tadpole was just about to leap off his bit of wood, when he caught sight of himself in the water. The pond was calm that day, like a mirror, and the tadpole could see himself well.

He stared down at himself in horror and amazement – for he did not see a tadpole, but a small frog!

"I've turned into a frog!" he croaked. "I have, I have! And all the other tadpoles are little frogs too! Why didn't I notice that before?"

"Tadpoles always turn into frogs. I could have told you that before, but you never would listen to anyone," said the stickleback. "Well – are you going to find the grass-snake and tell him to come and eat you and all your friends too? You said you would tell him where the frogs were in this pond."

But the tiny frog did not go to tell the snake anything. He felt quite certain that he would be eaten at once. He jumped into the pond with a splash, and swam as fast as he could to the other side of the water.

Wasn't he a silly fellow? He is five years old now, and quite grown-up – but you have only to say "Snake!" to him to send him leaping away in fright!

He was Clever After All!

THE little dog next door was always coming through the hedge into Robin's garden. He was black and brown, and he had a short, waggy tail and very nice brown eyes.

"I shall teach you tricks," said Robin to Wagger the dog. "There's a boy at school who has a marvellous dog. He can sit up and beg. He can shut the door. And he can even roll over and lie still on the ground, pretending to die for the queen!"

Wagger wagged his tail. He liked little boys very much. They nearly always had a thing called a ball, and Wagger loved a ball. He would run for miles round and round and up and down, if only he had a ball to chase.

But Wagger wasn't much good at learning tricks. He couldn't seem to sit up on his hind legs at all. He fell over at once.

"Wagger! Don't be so stupid!" said Robin. "Other dogs can sit up. Why can't you? Look, I'll hold you up for a bit – then I'll gently let go – and you'll find yourself sitting up beautifully. Just keep a nice straight back. Now – sit up! Beg!"

But Wagger fell over as soon as Robin took away his hand. It wasn't a bit of good.

"You're a stupid dog," said Robin, in disgust. "Mother, Wagger hasn't any brains at all. He's a dunce."

"He's too old to learn tricks," said Mother. "Dogs should learn when they are puppies, not when they are five years old, like Wagger."

Wagger looked longingly at the ball on the garden chair. What about a game, his brown eyes said, and he barked. "Wuff! What about a ball-game?"

"No. No game for you, because you haven't learnt a single trick," said Robin crossly. "And no biscuit either. Go back home. I don't want to play with a silly dog like you."

So Wagger went sadly back through the hedge. But he came to Robin the next day, still hoping to run after that ball.

"I'll just see if you are a bit cleverer today," said Robin, and he tried once more to teach Wagger a trick. But no, Wagger couldn't learn. He just didn't seem to understand at all. Robin got really very cross.

"You're not even trying! You're just being

stupid, Wagger. You must be the silliest dog in the world. I just won't play with you, or let you come into my garden any more! I'll block up the hole in the hedge."

So he did, and poor Wagger couldn't get through any more, and whined sadly. Why was that boy so cross with him? Wagger didn't understand.

Now, that afternoon Robin went to tea all by himself with his Granny. She lived quite a long way off, but Robin knew the way very well. He set off, and soon got there. He was pleased to see the lovely tea that Granny had got for him.

But, oh dear – when he set out to go home after tea, there was a thick fog everywhere! Robin went down the street and turned the corner. But after a bit, he stopped. Everywhere looked so different in a fog. He couldn't see the houses and shops he knew so well. If he wasn't careful he would be lost!

And very soon he *was* lost. He wandered about street after street, not meeting anyone, wondering where he was. Should he go to one of the houses and ask where he was? Would they think he was very silly? Oh dear, what a dreadful fog this was! Nobody, nobody would be able to find their way home, he was sure.

Suddenly he heard a patter of feet, and a little whine behind him. Then a bark. Wuff! Then a wet tongue touched his hand. Robin bent down and ran his hand over the little dog beside his knee.

"Wagger! Is it you?" he said, and Wagger barked joyfully. "Wuff, wuff! Yes, it's me!"

"Are you lost, too? Poor Wagger!" said Robin. "I'm quite, quite lost. I wish I could take you home, but I can't. I don't know the way. Wait a bit, Wagger. Don't leave me. I'd rather be lost with you than lost all by myself. I've got a bit of string. I'll slip it under your collar and you can keep close beside me. You may be the silliest dog in the world but you're a bit of company, anyway!"

Robin slipped the string under Wagger's collar. There – now he couldn't run off and leave him.

Wagger began to pull at the string, and Robin had to follow him. "Don't get us more lost, Wagger," begged Robin. "I'd better ask our way at one of these houses, I think."

But Wagger wouldn't stop. He went on and on, turning corners and crossing roads, and he pulled Robin along behind him.

"Stop, Wagger!" pulled Robin. "We'll be in

the next town soon, silly dog!"

Wagger suddenly stopped and pawed at a shut gate. And at the very same moment the door of the house opened, and somebody anxiously looked out. Robin saw who it was at once. His mother!

"Mother!" he shouted. "Oh, Mother! I was lost. I didn't know I was home, outside my own house. Oh, Mother – isn't Wagger clever, he's brought me all the way home by himself."

Wagger went indoors with Robin, wagging his tail. He didn't think he had done anything clever at all. A dog didn't need his eyes to see his way home – his nose would tell him! He had gone for a walk by himself and suddenly smelt Robin. Poor Robin, he had seemed upset, and Wagger had been glad to lead him safely home.

"Mother, I was wrong about Wagger. He isn't silly at all. He's very, very clever," said Robin. "And he's nice, too. I was horrid and cross to him, I even blocked up the hedge to stop him coming through – but when he found me, all lost by myself, he took me safely home. Mother, can I give him some biscuits?"

So, much to his surprise, Wagger had a wonderful feast of biscuits and was made a great fuss of, which pleased his loving, doggy heart very much. And the next day, what joy! Robin unblocked the hedge and called Wagger loudly.

"Wagger! Come and have a game of ball! Come on! No tricks, old fellow, but *ball*!"

And now Wagger plays ball each day with Robin, and you should see the clever way he chases it, and catches it in his mouth.

"You may be silly at some things," Robin says to him, "but you're very, very clever at others!"

The Lamb Without a Mother

ELLEN was staying at her uncle's farm. She liked being there, because there were so many nice things to do. She could feed the hens. She could take milk in a pail to the new calf. She could ride on Blackie, the old farm-horse.

It was winter-time, so it was not such fun as in the summer-time. But there was one great excitement – and that was the coming of the new lambs!

Ellen loved the baby lambs. The old shepherd lived in his hut on the hillside near the sheep, so that he could look after them when their lambs were born. Ellen often used to go and talk to him.

"Ah, it's a busy time with me," said the old shepherd. "Sometimes many lambs are born the same night, missy, and there are many babies to see to. You come and look at these two – a sweet pair they are!"

Ellen peeped into a little fold and saw a big mother-sheep there, with two tiny lambs beside her. Each of them had black noses, and they were butting them against their mother.

49

"I love them," said Ellen. "What do you feed them on, shepherd?"

"Oh, the mother feeds them," said the shepherd with a laugh. "Didn't you know, missy? Ah, yes, the lambs suck their mother's milk, and that's what makes them frisky and strong."

"What a good idea," said Ellen, and she watched the tiny lambs drinking their mother's milk. "Aren't they hungry, shepherd!"

"Little creatures always are," said the shepherd. "They have to grow big, you see, so they want a lot of food to build up their growing bodies. Birds bring grubs to their little ones, caterpillars eat the leaves of plants, young fish find their own food – and lambs drink their mother's milk."

One day, when Ellen went to see the old shepherd, she found him looking sad. "One of the mother-sheep has died," he said. "And she has left this little lamb behind her."

"Oh dear – and it has no mother to get milk from!" said Ellen sadly. "Will it die too?"

"I am going to see if another mother-sheep will take it," said the shepherd. "Maybe she will. She has only one lamb."

So he gave the tiny lamb to another sheep.

But she butted it away angrily.

"Isn't she unkind?" said Ellen, almost in tears. "She's got one lamb of her own, and surely she wouldn't mind having another. Most of the sheep have two."

"She isn't really unkind," said the shepherd. "She doesn't know the strange smell of this little lamb, so she doesn't like it. Well, well – she won't have it, that's plain!"

"What will you do?" asked Ellen.

"It will have to be fed from a baby's bottle," said the shepherd. "I shall put milk into a bottle, put a teat on it, and let the lamb suck. Then it will live."

Ellen stared at him in surprise. "Can you really feed a lamb out of a baby's bottle?" she said. "Oh, shepherd, please may I see you?"

"Of course," said the shepherd. He took out a glass bottle from his shed. He washed it, and then put some warm milk into it. He fitted a large teat on the end, and went to where he had left the tiny lamb.

He smeared the teat with milk and pushed it against the lamb's black nose. The tiny creature sniffed at it, and then put out its tongue and licked it.

"It likes the taste!" said Ellen in excitement.

"Oh, lamb, do drink the milk!"

The lamb opened his mouth and took hold of the milky teat. He sucked – for that is a thing that all lambs, all calves, all babies know how to do. He sucked hard.

The milk came through the teat and went into his mouth. The lamb sucked and sucked. He was hungry. The milk was nice. He sucked until he had nearly finished the bottle.

Ellen watched him in delight. "Please, please do let me hold the bottle whilst he finishes the few last drops," she begged the shepherd. So he gave her the bottle to hold.

Ellen loved feeding the tiny lamb. She liked

feeling him pulling hard at the bottle. He finished every drop of the milk, and licked the teat. Then he gave a sigh of happiness, as if to say, "That was really nice!"

"He'll do all right," said the shepherd, taking the empty bottle. "The pity is – I've no time to bottle-feed lambs just now."

"Shepherd – let me do it, then!" cried Ellen. "I know Uncle will let me. Can I go and ask him?"

The shepherd nodded, and Ellen sped off down the hill to where her uncle was working in the fields.

"Uncle! There's a lamb without a mother, so it hasn't any mother's milk to drink! The shepherd says it must be fed from a baby's bottle. Can I feed it for him every day, please, Uncle?"

"If you like," said her uncle. "It will need to be fed many times a day, Ellen, so you mustn't forget. You had better let the shepherd bring it down into the farmhouse garden for you. It can live there, and you can easily feed it from a bottle then, without climbing the hill every time."

Ellen ran to tell the shepherd. "You needn't carry it down for me," she said. "I can carry the little darling thing myself."

So she carried the little warm creature down to the garden. She shut the gate carefully so that it could not get out. It seemed to like being there, and frisked round happily.

Ellen fed it when it was hungry. Her aunt put milk into the baby's bottle, and Ellen went to take it to the lamb. He soon knew her and ran to meet her. How he sucked the milk from the bottle! He almost pulled it out of Ellen's hand sometimes!

He grew well. He had a tight, woolly coat to keep him warm, and a long wriggling tail. He could jump and spring about cleverly. Ellen often played with him in the garden, and they loved one another very much.

He grew quite fat and tubby. Ellen looked at him one day and said, "You are almost like a little sheep. Don't grow into a sheep, little lamb. Sheep never play. They just eat grass all day long, and say 'Baa-baa-baa'."

The lamb could bleat in his little high voice. Sometimes he would bleat for Ellen to bring him a bottle of milk. "Maa-maaa-maa!" he would say.

But soon there came a time when he did not need to drink milk any more. He could eat grass. He nibbled at it and liked it. Ellen watched him eating it, and was afraid that soon he would have to leave the garden and go into the big field with the others.

"Then you will forget about me, and won't come running to meet me any more," she said sadly.

One day the big sheep were sheared. The farmyard was full of their bleating, for they did not like their warm, thick woolly coats being cut away from them.

Ellen watched the shearing. "What a lot of wool!" she said. "I suppose that will be washed, and woven, and made into warm clothes. How useful the sheep are to us."

The lamb was not sheared. He was allowed to keep his coat that year. "It is not thick enough for shearing," said the shepherd. "The lambs keep their coats. They will be very thick next year. And now, missy, I think your lamb must come and live in the field. He is old enough to be with the others, now that you have quite finished feeding him by bottle."

Ellen was sad. She took the little lamb from the farmhouse garden to the field. She opened the gate and let him through. He stood quite still and stared at all the sheep and lambs there.

Then a small lamb came up to him. "Come and play 'Jump-high, jump-low' with us," he said. "It's such fun."

The little lamb frisked off in delight. "He has forgotten me already," said Ellen.

But he hadn't. Whenever the little girl goes by the field, the lamb comes running up to the hedge, bleating. He pushes his nose through, and Ellen pats him. And I expect that he will always remember his little friend, and run happily to greet her, don't you?

The Tail that Broke Off

"I am a very pretty little lizard," said Blinky, looking at himself in a tiny puddle. "I have bright eyes, and a lovely orange patch underneath my brown body, and a nice long tail."

"Don't be vain," said Runabout, his sister. "You are always thinking about yourself, Blinky. You will be sorry one day!"

Then the slow-worm slid up and spoke to the vain little lizard. "Pride comes before a fall," he said. "Nasty things happen to people who think too much of themselves!"

"Who is going to take any notice of a stupid creature like *you*?" said Blinky rudely. "You're only a worm, a slow-worm!"

"I'm *not* a worm," said the slow-worm crossly. "I have a silly name, I know. But I'm not a worm, and I'm not slow, and I'm not blind or deaf either!"

"Well, if you're not a worm, what are you?" asked Blinky, surprised. "Are you a snake?"

"Of course not!" said the slow-worm, getting crosser. "Can't you see that I can blink my eyes, just as you can? You know quite well that a snake has no eyelids and can't shut its eyes. And look at my tongue. It isn't forked in two, as a snake's tongue is."

The slow-worm put out his tongue, and the lizard saw that it was just notched at the end, not forked. Blinky knew that he and his brothers and sisters had a tongue like that too, and he stared in surprise at the slow-worm.

"Well, surely you are not a lizard like *us*, are you?" he cried. "You haven't any legs."

"I know," said the slow-worm. "But I belong to the lizard family, all the same, not to the snakes or the worms! So just you be polite to me, Blinky, or something horrid will happen to you!"

"Pooh!" said Blinky. "That's what everyone says, but nothing *does* happen!"

"Blinky! Run to your hole, quickly!" suddenly cried Runabout, his sister. "I am sure there is danger near!"

Blinky raised himself up on his pretty little fingers, and listened, his head up in the air. He could hear nothing.

Runabout ran away. The slow-worm began to slide away too. "You'd better go, Blinky," he said. "There is danger about. I can smell it!"

"They all think they know so much better

than I do!" said Blinky. "I can't hear anything! I can't see or smell any danger at all."

But there *was* danger, all the same. The big grey rat was about that morning. He was hungry. He was fierce. He didn't mind whether he ate a baby bird, a lizard, a mouse, or even one of the flies that the lizards liked. He came slinking between the heather, stopping to listen every now and again.

He heard the rustle of Blinky's body against the heather, and he listened again. Then he ran out to where the vain little lizard still stood, and pounced on him.

Blinky tried to dart away – but the rat had him by the tail. "Let me go!" squealed poor Blinky. "Let me go!"

But the rat was not going to let him go. Here was a nice dinner, and he was going to eat it.

Blinky was stiff with fear. His whole body went tight and hard, and suddenly a dreadful thing happened. He pulled hard, trying to get away from the rat – and his beautiful tail broke right off!

Yes, it really did. It broke off, and Blinky ran away into his hole, a poor, tailless lizard, ugly and strange.

He left his tail behind him. The rat let it go

in surprise, when it broke off, and made as if to go after the running lizard. But the broken-off tail began to act in such a strange way that the rat stopped to watch.

It jumped about as if it was alive! The rat watched in surprise. Then he pounced on the funny, jerking tail, and ate it in two or three bites.

Then he looked for Blinky. But by that time the little lizard had gone. He was lying in his hole, trembling and shaking.

"The slow-worm said something would happen to me," he said to himself. "He did, he did! And now something *has* happened! I've lost my tail. It broke itself off. Oh, how strange I shall look without my beautiful tail! How all the other lizards will laugh at me! And so will the slow-worm!"

Poor little Blinky. He was very unhappy. He didn't go out into the sunshine he loved, but he stayed in his hole all day. A fly crawled in, and he ate it. But that was all the food he had.

Runabout, his sister, came to find him. "What is the matter, Blinky?" she asked. "Did the rat frighten you? He is gone now. Come out and play."

"No," said Blinky. "I can't. I have lost my

tail. I look dreadful – so short and ugly."

"Blinky! Lost your tail! How did you do that?" asked Runabout in surprise.

"The rat caught me by the tail, and when I pulled away from him, my body went stiff, and my tail broke off," said Blinky. "The rat ate it. I heard him gobbling it up. Oh, Runabout, I am so sad. I shall never come out and play again. Never, never! I wish it was cold weather, time to go and sleep all day and night, then nobody would know about my tail."

"But, Blinky, you must feed yourself, or you will die," said Runabout. "Come along out. We will all be kind to you."

"No, I feel too much ashamed of myself," said Blinky. "I was so vain. I thought such a lot of myself, and everyone said something would happen to me! And now it has."

"Well, if you won't come out and play, and catch flies for your dinner, I will look after you," said kind little Runabout. "I will catch as many flies as I can, Blinky, and give them to you for your food."

"Thank you," said Blinky. So Runabout went out into the sunshine, running here and there on her tiny little fingers and toes, catching any fly she saw.

Some she ate herself, some she took to Blinky in his hole. She did not take him as many as he would have caught for himself, so he grew a little thin.

He would not come out of his hole. He stayed there day after day, lonely and unhappy. He had asked Runabout not to tell anyone about his lost tail. He was so ashamed.

"If only I hadn't been so silly and vain," he thought. "I know everyone will laugh at me, and the slow-worm would say that it served me right. I couldn't bear it. It is bad enough to be without a tail."

The lizards soon forgot about Blinky. Runabout was the only one who remembered him, and she took him flies twenty times a day. The little lizard gobbled them up, for he was always hungry.

One day the slow-worm came again to the lizard's sunny playground in the heather. He looked round for Blinky, but he could not see him. "Where is Blinky?" he asked Runabout.

"He's in his hole, and he has been there for a very long time," said Runabout.

"Why?" asked the slow-worm.

"Well," said Runabout, "the rat pounced on him, and his tail broke off. He was so ashamed of his short, ugly body that he hid himself away. I can't get him out of his hole."

"Silly fellow!" said the slow-worm, and glided away to find Blinky. He went into the hole and spoke to him.

"Come along into the sunshine. It is bad for you to lie here alone like that. It would be better for you to come out and be laughed at, than lie here, sad and lonely."

"I have no tail," said poor Blinky. The slow-worm slid to the back of the hole to look at Blinky's short body. He gave a squeak.

"But you *have* a tail! Yes, you have, Blinky! It's not so fine as your first tail, but still, it's a tail! Come into the sun and let us all see it."

In great excitement Blinky ran into the sunshine, and the slow-worm called all the other lizards to him.

"Look! Look! Blinky has grown a new tail! Isn't it marvellous?"

"It's not so fine as his first one," said Runabout. "And it doesn't seem to join on very well – it's not a tail that fits you properly, Blinky. But still, it *is* a tail and you look quite all right. You'll never look as beautiful as you did, Blinky, but perhaps you will be nicer now."

Blinky was full of joy. He had a new tail! It wasn't so long or so nice as the other one – but still, he had a tail of his own. He had grown it and, how queer, he hadn't known it. How marvellous!

"All lizards can grow new tails if their old ones break off," said the slow-worm wisely. "I could grow one, too, if I broke mine. Snakes can't, but lizards can. I'm glad I'm a lizard. If any enemy comes after me, I shall break off my tail and escape, like Blinky did. It was clever of you, Blinky."

"No, it wasn't," said Blinky. "I am not going to let you say it was. My tail broke off by itself. *I* was too slow to escape the rat – but my tail was quick enough to snap and let me run away! It's my tail that is clever, not I!"

Blinky was nicer after that. He wasn't vain any more. He still has his new tail. You'll know him if you see him, because you can see where it grew on to his body. Wasn't it a good thing he got another?

Susan and the Birds

SUSAN was very fond of the birds in the garden. She badly wanted to get near to them and watch them. But whenever she crept close, they flew away.

"It's such a pity, Mummy," she said. "I only want to watch them, and see how pretty they are, and find out what bird sings so sweetly –but they won't let me, they keep flying away. Don't they know I'm their friend?"

"Well, no, they don't, darling," said her mother. "You see, most people don't bother about watching the birds, they just frighten them away – so they think you are the same."

"But I'm not," said Susan. "I want to be friends with them – but they won't be friends with me!"

"Well, you must make them tame," said her mother. "Then they will let you come near them."

"How can I do that?" asked Susan.

"We will give them a bird-table," said her mother. "They will love that. It is winter-time now, and all the birds that eat insects are hungry, because there are so few flies and grubs to be found. They will soon come to your table, and then you can watch them closely."

So Mother made Susan a bird-table. It was very easy to make. First Mother took a square piece of board. That was for the top of the table. Then she found an old broom-handle. That was for the leg. She nailed the square bit of board to the broom-handle, and then drove the other end of the handle into the ground.

"There's your table for the birds!" she said to Susan. "If you put out bits of food each day, you will soon make friends with the birds!"

The table was very near Susan's playroom window. She was pleased. "I can sit in the window and watch the birds hop on to the table easily," she said. "Mummy, what shall I put on it? Anything else besides food?"

"Well, the birds would like a few twigs nailed behind the table, I think," said Mother. "Then they can perch on those when they fly down. And you should put a bowl of water out too, Susan. They have to drink as well as eat – and on a nice fine day they may have a bath in it."

Susan couldn't help feeling excited. She put a bowl of water on the table and then she found a few nice twigs in the hedge. With her little hammer and a few nails, she nailed the twigs to the back of the table. Now it was ready!

"What do the birds like to eat?" she asked. "I know some of them like insects, but I can't give them those. Most of them like soaked bread, don't they, Mummy?"

"Yes. You can give them that – and any crumbs from the tablecloth and bread-bin – and the scrapings from the milk-pudding dish," said Mother.

So Susan put those out on the bird-table. Then she went into her playroom, hid behind the curtain and watched.

The sparrows saw the food there first. They talked about it in the trees nearby, and wondered if they dared to go down and try it.

"There is no cat about," said a brown sparrow. "Let's go. I'll fly down first and then chirrup to you if it is safe."

So he flew down to the twigs at the back of the bird-table, and had a look at the food. It looked very good to him! He flew down on to the table and pecked at the bread.

"The first bird on my table!" said Susan in joy. "What a little dear he is, with his brown coat and dark head!"

"Chirrup, chirrup!" said the sparrow, and at

once two or three more flew down to peck at the soaked bread. Soon the table was quite full of the noisy little birds.

Susan pressed her nose close to the window-pane. The birds saw her, and flew away in fright. But another little bird flew down at once, and gave a little trill.

"Oh – a robin!" said Susan. "A lovely red-breast. Look at his red breast, Mummy, and his bright black eyes, and long thin legs. Isn't he lovely? And oh, listen to him!"

The robin pecked at the bits of milk pudding and the bread. When two or three sparrows flew down again he flew off. "He doesn't like to mix with the noisy sparrows," said Mother, who had come to watch too. "Ah, look – here's a lovely big bird, Susan. What is it?"

"A blackbird of course!" said Susan. "Every-one knows *him*!"

He was a black, glossy fellow, much bigger than the sparrows. He drove them away and began to peck up the bread and the pudding greedily. Whilst he was eating it a bird as big as he was flew down and joined him.

It was brown and had speckles all over its chest. "What is it?" asked Susan.

"A thrush of course!" said Mother. "Look

at the freckles on his breast. You can always tell a thrush by those – and both he and the blackbird have lovely songs too. You will hear them in the spring-time."

"That's four different kinds of birds already," said Susan. "Oh, Mummy, my bird-table *is* going to be fun!"

"We'll put something else on the table tomorrow," said Mother. "Then one or two other birds will come."

So the next day Mother gave Susan two bones, one to hang from the table and the other to put *on* the table.

"Why should I hang one on string?" asked Susan.

"For the tits," said Mother. "They like to swing on their food – so they can swing on this bone. But the big starlings like to stand on their bone – so you can just lay that one on the table for them."

It was great fun to watch for the little tits and the starlings. The tits came first. They were pretty little birds, with blue caps on their heads, and blue and yellow coats.

"Blue-tits," said Mother. "You may perhaps see the great-tit too. He wears a black cap, and is bigger, so you will know him when he comes.

See how those blue-tits stand upside down on their bone and swing to and fro. Aren't they enjoying it!"

It was fun to watch the tits – but it was even more fun to watch the starlings. They were bigger than the tits and sparrows, but not so big as the blackbird. They were greedy, noisy, bad-mannered birds, dressed in feathers that shone blue and green and purple.

"Oh, look how they peck one another, and call each other rude names!" said Susan. "Oh, Mummy, that one has pushed the other off the table! No – he's back again – and he's pushed the first one off the bone – and now a third one is trying his hardest to drag the bone away!"

The starlings chattered and squawked, pecked and quarrelled. It was really funny to watch them. Some sparrows came down to join in the fun, and the blackbird turned up, but flew away because the table was too crowded.

"I do like my bird-table!" said Susan. "It's the greatest fun, Mummy. The birds don't seem to mind me peeping at them now, either. They must know that I put the food out for them!"

The birds sipped the water, and once the robin had a bath in it. He splashed the water all over himself.

"Now we will put out something for a few seed-eating birds, said Mummy. "I would like you to see the pretty chaffinch, Susan. He will come if we get a few seeds for him."

So they bought a mixture of bird-seed and put some on the table. The sparrows found the seeds at once and pecked them up greedily.

"Their beaks are very good for breaking up the seeds," said Susan, watching them. "They have big strong beaks, haven't they, Mummy?"

"So has the chaffinch, if only he would come and show us his beak!" said Mother. "Ah, there he is! Now see how pretty he is, Susan, with his bright pink breast, and the white bars on his wings, that flash when he flies!"

"Pink pink!" said the chaffinch, as he flew down to the table for the first time. "Seeds for me! Pink pink!"

He took some in his strong beak and cracked them well. Susan saw that he had just the same kind of beak as the sparrows, but he was a neater, prettier bird. His little wife flew down to the table too, but she hadn't his beautiful pink breast.

"Mummy, I know heaps of birds now," said Susan. "And I shall get to know lots more, shan't I? Mummy, do you think the birds are pleased with their bird-table?"

"Very pleased," said Mother. "And they will pay you back for your kindness in the spring, Susan!"

They did! The thrush sang his song over and over again to her. The blackbird fluted in his wonderful voice. The robin sang in little trills. The chaffinch carolled loudly. It was wonderful to hear them all!

"Thank you!" said Susan. "You have paid me well for your table!"

Do have a table for the birds too. You will love it just as much as Susan did.

What a Silly Thing To Do!

WHENEVER John came in from school, he took off his cap, coat, gloves and scarf and threw them on the floor for somebody else to pick up!

"John! How many times have I told you not to do that!" said his mother. "Pick up your things. They get so dirty and creased on the floor."

It was the same at bedtime. Down on the floor went all John's things! And if you looked into his drawers, what an untidy mess you would see there. Even if his mother had tidied them that very morning, they would all be in a jumble again by the evening.

He couldn't remember to shut gates when he went into a field. He couldn't remember to shut the door behind him – and if he did, he usually banged it.

"Can't you possibly teach John to be tidier and more careful?" his Aunt Sarah said to his mother. "Really dear, when he comes to tea with me, he is dreadful – leaves my front gate

open so that the hens walk all over my garden
– leaves the larder door open if he fetches
something, so that the cat gets in and eats
everything – and flings his things about all over
the place!"

"Well, Sarah, I've done my best," said his
mother with a sigh. "He just won't be taught!"

"I've got two or three children coming to tea
with me next week," said Aunt Sarah. "John
can come too if he likes – on Tuesday – but tell
him to behave himself or I shan't ask him
again."

John was pleased to go to his aunt's because
she always had lovely teas, and she was a very
jolly person too, although she scolded him well
when he deserved it.

"Your aunt has three dear little puppies, she
says," said his mother. "You'll love playing
with them."

So John looked forward to Tuesday and was
glad when it came. "You can wear your new
coat," said Mother, "and look, here is a scarf
and gloves I have knitted for you – they match
and you will look fine in them."

They were red. John was very pleased. He
put on his new coat, wound his scarf round his
neck, pulled on his gloves and put on his cap.

"Yes, you look very nice," said his mother. "Now be careful of all your new things. And look – take this basket to Aunt Sarah, with my love. It's a special shortbread I baked for her and Uncle Fred, and a pound of the sausages she likes."

John set off, swinging the basket. When he came to his aunt's, he saw Nell, the big collie dog, in the field with her puppies. They were having a fine time together. The hens pecked about, and took no notice of the puppies. They were used to them.

John opened the gate and went to see the puppies. How he loved them! He stayed far too long with them, and suddenly heard his aunt calling. "John! John! The others have been here a long time. Hurry up and come in. We are just sitting down to tea."

"Coming!" yelled John. "I've got some shortbread for you, Auntie, and a pound of sausages."

"Put them in the larder for me!" called his aunt.

He ran out of the field. He didn't shut the gate as he ought to have done. He ran to his aunt's house and went in. He took off his cap, scarf, gloves and coat and flung them down on the floor as usual. What a dreadful boy!

He smelt a nice smell of hot toast. He couldn't wait to put the shortbread and the sausages into the larder, so he put them down on the floor in the basket, and ran into his aunt's room to have tea.

"Hallo, John!" said everyone. "Did you see the puppies? Aren't they sweet?"

John had left the front door open as well as the field gate, and because of this a dreadful thing happened. The puppies trotted out of the field gate. About seven hens followed too. They all came to the house and saw the front door open.

In they went, and the first thing the puppies smelt was the cake and the sausages! The hungry little things pulled them out of the basket on the floor, and began to have a lovely time. Gobble, gobble, gobble, chew, chew, chew! What a fine mixture shortbread and sausages were!

The hens pecked up all the crumbs. They clucked with joy. This was a treat!

Then the puppies saw all John's clothes on the floor. Good. Here was something else to eat! So they began to chew at the coat and the cap, the scarf and the gloves! They chewed the fingers off the gloves. They pulled the fringe off the scarf. They bit big holes in the coat-sleeves. Oh, they had a wonderful time, and made funny little growly noises as they played.

The children heard them. "What's that noise?" said Gladys. "It sounds like the puppies – and a few hens too!"

"Go and see, John," said his aunt, so out he went. What a terrible sight he saw! There were bits of red wool and bits of sausage and bits of shortbread scattered all over the place. He stood and wailed out loud.

"Oh, Auntie Sarah! Oh, quick, do come! Oh, Auntie, Auntie, the puppies and the hens have eaten what I brought you, and they're gobbling up my clothes!"

His aunt raced out at once. She stood still in horror when she saw what had happened. "Who left the field gate open? Who left the front door open so that the pups could get in? Did you leave your things on the floor again, John? And why didn't you put the basket in the larder as I told you?"

"Grrrr!" said a puppy, and tore a bit out of the scarf. Slap! Smack! Biff! Auntie Sarah's hand came down on the surprised puppies, and they yelped loudly.

"Oh, don't smack them!" cried John, who couldn't bear to see the puppies slapped. "Oh, Auntie, don't!"

But Auntie did. She gave each of the puppies a good smack, and they fled away to the field, with their little tails well down.

"They have been naughty," said Auntie. "It's true that it was your fault that they were naughty, John, for you left open the gate and the door, and you left your things on the floor again where the puppies could get them. They have been punished because of you. I really feel ashamed of you."

John was very sad indeed. He didn't go back to finish his tea. He felt as if he couldn't play with the puppies that day, because it was he who had caused them to be smacked. He put on his spoilt clothes, took the empty basket and ran home. His mother was surprised to see him – and how angry and upset she was to see his spoilt clothes.

"Oh, Mother, Auntie ought to have smacked me, not the puppies," sobbed John. "It was all my fault. Oh, I do feel so bad about it."

"I should think so," said his mother. "I feel bad about it too – after all the trouble I took to

78

get you nice new things. Now you will have to wear your old things again."

"What can I do to put things right?" said John. "Can I take some money out of my money-box to buy some more wool for you? Can I buy more shortbread and sausages?"

"I'll tell you what you can do," said his mother. "You can make up your mind to be tidy and careful in future. That will please me and your aunt, and will soon put things right, because we shall be proud of you, instead of ashamed. See what you can do."

John never forgot that the puppies had been punished for something that was his fault. He always shuts gates and doors now and puts things away properly. But what a horrid way it was to learn that lesson! Poor John.

Hoppitty-Skip and Crawl-About

HOPPITTY-SKIP was a frog. He could jump very high in the air, because his hind legs were long and strong.

One day he leapt high, and came down plop – but not on the ground! He had jumped on to the back of a toad!

"Crrr-oak!" said the toad crossly. "Look where you are going!"

"Oh, I'm sorry," said the frog, jumping off the toad's back quickly. "You are so like a clod of earth that I didn't see you."

"I suppose I am," said the toad. "It is a good idea to hide from enemies by looking exactly like the ground. Where are you going?"

"I am going to the pond," said the frog. "I think it is time I found a wife and had some eggs laid in the pond."

"I shall soon be doing the same," said the toad. "I always go to the pond at the bottom of this field."

"Oh, that's a long way away," said the frog. "I go to the little pond near by."

"Don't go there this year," said the toad. "There are ducks on it."

"Well, I will come to your pond, then," said the frog.

"In a short time the frog had found a mate, and she had laid her eggs in a big mass of jelly in the pond. The toad, too, had eggs, but they were not in a mass – they were in a double-string of jelly, wound in and out of the water-weeds.

"My eggs rise up to the surface where the sun can warm them," said the frog. "Look – you can see the tiny black specks wriggling in the jelly. They are tadpoles already."

Soon there were both frog and toad tadpoles in the pond. They wriggled about and had a lovely time.

"Let us leave the pond now," said the frog to the toad. "I am tired of all these wriggling tadpoles. We will go and find a nice damp place somewhere in a ditch."

So they left the warm pond and made their way to a ditch the toad knew. The frog went by leaps and bounds, but the toad didn't. He either crawled, or did some funny little hops that made the frog laugh.

"Why don't you leap along like me?" he said.

"You're so slow."

"I am not made like you," said the toad. "I am heavier and my legs are shorter. Anyway, why do you leap along so quickly? It is a hot day. Go slowly."

"I can't help jumping," said the frog. "And besides, Crawl-About, my high leaps are very useful to me sometimes, when enemies are near."

"I don't believe it," said Crawl-About. "It is much wiser to crouch on the ground and pretend to be a clod of earth, as I do."

Just then a rat came by and saw the frog and the toad. The toad sank to the earth and seemed to vanish, he was so like the soil. The rat pounced on the frog – but at once the little creature rose high in the air, and the rat ran back, startled. By the time he had come back again to find the frog, Hoppitty-Skip had vanished into some long grass.

He waited until the rat had gone. Then he looked for his friend. He could not see him at all – and then suddenly he saw the toad's beautiful coppery eyes looking at him near by. He was still crouching on the ground, so like it that the frog could only make out his shining eyes.

"Well, did you see how I startled the rat?" asked the frog in delight. "Didn't I make him jump? I just had time to vanish into the long grass."

"Well, your way of dealing with enemies is good for you, and mine is good for me," said the toad, beginning to crawl again. "We all have our different ways, Hoppitty-Skip. Mine is to crouch down and keep still, yours is to jump. I have another way of getting the better of an enemy too."

"What's that?" asked the frog. But the toad had no breath to tell him.

They found a good place in a ditch. The long grass was damp there, and both the creatures liked that. They did not like dryness. They sat and waited for food to come to them. The toad fell asleep.

The frog had a lovely time. A big bluebottle fly came along and perched on a leaf just above the frog's head. Out flicked his tongue – and the fly was gone! The frog blinked his eyes and swallowed.

He waited for another fly to come. But the next thing that came along was a fat green caterpillar, arching its back as it crawled.

Out flicked the frog's tongue – and the surprised caterpillar disappeared down the frog's throat.

"I say!" said a little mouse near by. "I say, Hoppitty-Skip – how do you manage to catch flies and grubs so easily? You must have a very long tongue!"

"I've a very clever sort of tongue," said the frog, and he flicked it out to show the mouse. "Look, it's fastened to the front of my mouth, instead of the back, as yours is. So I can flick it out much farther!"

He flicked it out again and hit the mouse on the nose with it. "Don't," said the mouse.

"Your tongue feels sticky. Look – there's another fly!"

A big fly was buzzing just above their heads. The frog flicked out his long tongue, and flicked it back again. The fly was stuck on the end of his tongue, and went down his throat! "Most delicious," said the frog. "It's a very great pity old Crawl-About sleeps all the day – he misses such a lot of good meals!"

Crawl-About woke up at night. He gave a croak and set out on a walk. "Where are you going?" called the frog, who wanted to sleep. "You'll lose your way in the dark."

"No, I shan't," said the toad. "I never do. I always know my way back easily. I am off to find a few slugs, a score or so of beetles, and maybe even a baby mouse if I can get one. I'll be back by the morning."

Sure enough, he was back in his place by the morning, though he had crawled and hopped quite a long way in the night. He told Hoppitty-Skip that he had had a very good time, and eaten so many things that all he wanted to do now was to sleep.

"You are not really very good company," said the frog. "You like to sleep all day and wander off at night. Well, well – all the more flies for me, I suppose!"

The frog's body was smooth and fresh-looking. The toad's was pimply and dark, much drier than the frog's. The frog thought he had much the nicer body of the two, and he was glad he had quick legs and a high bound. It was fun to be in the field that hot summer weather. It was always moist in the ditch.

One day the rat came back again. The frog gave a great leap and got away. The toad crouched down flat as before. But the raw saw him and pounced fiercely on him.

"Now he'll be eaten!" said Hoppitty-Skip, in fright. "Oh, what a pity he hasn't a good high jump as I have, then he could get away quickly."

But the toad had yet another way in which he could get rid of an enemy. From his pimply body he sent out some nasty-smelling, nasty-tasting stuff. The rat got a taste of it and drew back, his mouth open in disgust.

"Eat me if you like," croaked the toad, "but I shall be the most horrible-tasting meal you have ever had! I may even poison you. Lick me, rat – taste me! Do you still think you would like me for a meal?"

The rat fled, still with his mouth wide open.

He couldn't bear the evil taste on his tongue. Oh, he would never, never pounce on a toad again!

"Are you there, Hoppitty-Skip?" asked Crawl-About. "Don't look so frightened. I am quite all right. Your trick of leaping is very good – but my trick of hiding, and of sending out nasty-tasting stuff all over my back, is even better!"

Soon the cold days came. "I must get back to the pond," said the frog. "Come with me, Crawl-About. Come and sleep in the mud with me. We shall be safe there all through the winter."

"I might," said the toad sleepily. "Go and have a look at the pond and see if it is very crowded."

The frog went, and soon came hopping back. The toad was under a big stone. The frog peeped beneath it.

"Come to the pond," he said. "There is plenty of room. I have found two good places in the mud at the bottom."

But there was no answer. The toad had already gone to sleep for the winter! Nothing would wake him. He slept soundly under his stone, looking like a dark piece of earth.

"Well, there's no waking him," said Hoppitty-Skip. "Good-bye, Crawl-About. I'm off to sleep in the pond. See you again in the spring!"

And off he hopped to sleep the cold days and nights away, tucked into the mud at the bottom of the pond. You won't be able to see him in the winter – but you might find Crawl-About. Don't disturb him, will you.

Freckles For a Thrush

AN ELF once came to the garden where the thrush lived. He was a clever little elf, and the thrush used to love to watch him at work.

He painted the tips of the daisy-petals bright crimson and spots on the ladybirds. He even painted the blackbird's beak a bright orange-gold for him in the spring.

The thrush was rather tiresome. He was always asking questions, always poking his beak here and there, always upsetting pots of paint.

The elf got angry with him. "Look here, you big clumsy bird, don't come near me any more!" he said. "I'm going to be very busy just now, painting mauve and green on the starling's feathers. If you keep disturbing me I shall get the colours wrong."

But the thrush couldn't leave the little painter alone. He always had to peep and see what he was doing. Then one day he spied a worm just by the elf and darted at it. He pulled it up and upset half a dozen paint pots at once.

The colours all ran together on the grass, and the elf groaned.

"Look there! Half my colours wasted! That blue was for the blue-tit's cap – and that yellow was for the celandines in spring. I detest you, thrush. Go away!"

"I don't see why you should waste your lovely colours on stupid birds like the starling and the blue-tit," said the thrush. "They have nice feathers already. What about *me*? I am a dull brown bird with no colour at all, not even a bright beak! Won't you paint *me*, elfin painter – that would be a kind and sensible thing to do."

"I don't want to be kind and sensible to you," said the elf. "I don't like you. Go away!"

"Yes, but elf, I do think you might spare me a little of your . . ." began the tiresome thrush again, and trod on the painter's biggest brush and broke it.

"*Now* look what you've done!" shouted the elf, in a rage, and he shook the brush he was using at the thrush. A shower of brown drops of paint flew all over the front of the surprised thrush, and stuck there.

"Oh – you've splashed my chest with your brown paint!" said the thrush crossly. "I shall complain to the head-brownie in the wood. He will punish you!"

He flew off – but the head-brownie only laughed. "It serves you right, anyhow!" he said. "And why complain, thrush? Didn't you want your coat to be made brighter? Well, I think your freckled breast is very, very pretty. Go and look at yourself in the pond."

The thrush went and looked into the water. Yes! He looked fine with his speckly, freckly breast. He liked it enormously. He flew back to thank the elfin painter, but he had collected his pots and gone off in a temper.

I like the freckles on the thrush, too. Do you? You might go and look at him. He's very proud of his freckles now.

The Very Strange Chicks

ONCE there was a hen who wanted to sit on eggs. The farmer's wife was pleased.

"Here is a hen who wants to sit on eggs every day and night!" she said. "We will give her some duck's eggs to sit on. The duck is a bad mother. She will not sit on her eggs!"

So the farmer's wife took twelve duck's eggs, and put them in a nest of straw. She set the old brown hen on the greeny-blue eggs, and the big bird settled down at once. She was happy.

"This is what I wanted!" she said to her friend, the white hen. "I wanted to feel a lot of eggs under me. I wanted to cover them, and keep them warm. I am happy now."

Her friend was sitting on eggs too, but they were hen's eggs, not duck's. Both the birds were happy. They loved sitting on the big clutches of eggs.

They sat on them for many days. Sometimes they left them for a little while to pick up some grain, or to have a drink of water. But they soon went back, fluffed themselves out well, and covered the eggs with their feathers and moist warm bodies.

"We must not let them get cold or too dry," said the white hen.

"If we do, they will not hatch out into little chicks," said the brown hen. "Cluck-cluck. We will keep them very warm."

One day the white hen was excited. She bent her head down and listened.

"What is the matter?" said the brown hen.

"My eggs are going to hatch!" said the white hen. "I can hear one little chick tapping with his beak inside the egg. Soon it will break – and I shall see a dear little fluffy chick!"

The white hen was right. Before the next morning, all her eggs were hatched. She had twelve dear little chicks. Six of them were bright yellow, and six of them were a mixture of brown and yellow. They ran about, and cheeped in little high voices.

Then the eggs of the brown hen hatched too. Out came, not chicks, but twelve little ducklings. They were all bright yellow. The hen was very pleased with them. She thought they were chicks, and she clucked to them lovingly.

"Dear little chicks of mine! I will take care of you! When you hear me call sharply, like this – CLUCK-CLUCK – you must run to me at once, and hide under my wings."

The chicks and the ducklings knew their own mother hens. The chicks always ran to the white hen when she called them, and the ducklings always ran to the brown hen.

Sometimes the cat came into the farmyard, and the hens would cluck loudly. "An enemy is near! CLUCK-CLUCK! Come here, come here, an enemy is near!"

Then the little chicks would run to the white hen and hide under her feathers, and the little ducklings would run to the brown hen.

It was funny to see their heads peeping out from the feathers of the hens. First one little head would pop out and then another and another, until it seemed as if each hen had one big head and many little ones!

The hens tried to teach their little ones all the things they should know. "This is the way to scratch the ground, to see if any grain of corn is buried there," the white hen would say to her chicks. And she scratched at the earth with her short, strong legs, and big, blunt claws.

Then she would peck up a grain of corn with her strong beak. She was very good at scratching with her feet, and pecking with her beak.

Sometimes, when a chick was naughty, she would give him a sharp peck. Then he would be good again for quite a long while.

It was a happy time in the farmyard for the little chicks and ducks. The sun was warm. There were many things to see and hear. There was the old sow, grunting in her sty. There were the great big cows that came to the milking-shed. There were the white ducks that waddled to the round pond.

The ducklings grew fast, and so did the chicks. They ran with one another, and cheeped in their high voices. It was fun in the farmyard, and there were always their mothers to run to if they were afraid of anything.

One day the ducklings saw the pond. One duckling had gone after the ducks, when they had waddled to the pond, and he had suddenly seen the big stretch of water.

"What is it? What is it?" he cheeped. He ran to the other chicks and ducklings, and made them come with him to see this wonderful new thing.

"Pooh!" said the chicks. "What a thing to bring us here to see! Just water!"

"Is that what it is? Water!" said the ducklings, who were most excited to see the pond.

"Yes," said the biggest chick. "You had better come away from it. Our mothers say it is not good for us."

"But it looks lovely! It looks very, very good! We love it!" said all the little yellow ducklings, and one of them took a step nearer.

The brown hen saw him. "CLUCK-CLUCK-CLUCK!" she cried. "Bad little chick! Come here at once. How dare you go near that dreadful pond!"

She ran at the ducklings, and chased them away from the water. But they did not forget it.

One morning it rained so hard that a big puddle was made in the farmyard. The ducklings found it and waddled into it joyfully. Oh, how lovely it felt!

The brown hen saw them, and she was very angry indeed. "How dare you get your feet wet?" she said. "You bad little chicks! How dare you get wet? Don't you know that chicks never get wet if they can help it?"

But the ducklings loved the puddle, and they were very sorry when it dried up.

"Let's go and find that pond again," said the biggest duckling. "I want to get my feet wet. I want to get right into the water. I want to paddle in it."

All the ducklings felt the same. The chicks would not come with them. "What! Go into that horrid, wet, cold water! Get our feet wet and our feathers damp?" they cheeped. "Of course not!"

So the ducklings went alone. They came to the pond. They stood by the edge. They put their little feet into the water, and it felt lovely.

The brown hen came rushing up. "Come away at once, at once, at once! Come away! CLUCK-CLUCK-CLUCK!"

But this time the ducklings did not listen to her. One duckling jumped straight into the pond – splash! And then another and another went in – splash, splash, splash! They were all

in, and swimming beautifully, their little webbed feet paddling along, pushing themselves forward! It was sweet to see them.

The old mother hen was afraid for them. She ran up and down the bank of the pond, squawking so loudly that the farmer's wife came out to see what was the matter.

"Oh!" she said. "Poor old mother hen –your babies have gone into the pond. But don't worry – they are not chicks, but ducklings!"

"Cluck, cluck!" said the hen, in great surprise. She had always thought they were chicks.

"They are made for swimming in the water," said the farmer's wife. She called one of her big white ducks to her. "See," she said to the anxious hen, "the duck's feet are made for swimming – they have webbed skin between the toes. Yours are not webbed, but they are strong to help you to scratch for grain. You have strong claws too, to help you."

"Cluck-cluck!" said the hen, beginning to understand.

"Look at the duck's beak," said the farmer's wife. "It is quite different from yours, henny-penny! It is flat and hollow; and do you see these les? They let out the water and the mud when the duck dives into the mud to hunt for water-insects. The insects are left behind in the duck's beak, and she eats them – but the water and the mud drain out!"

"Cluck-cluck!" said the hen.

"Chicks will be hens and ducklings will be ducks," said the farmer's wife, letting the duck waddle away. "Ducks will always waddle, because their legs are put so far back to help them to swim well. Hens will always run and scratch."

"Cluck-cluck!" said the hen, listening.

"Hens will always peck up their grain, and ducks will always shovel their beaks in the mud," said the farmer's wife. "That is why you have such different beaks. Don't scold your babies, henny-penny. It is me you should scold, because I gave you duck's eggs to sit on, instead of hen's eggs!"

"Cluck-cluck!" said the hen, and stared at her little babies swimming on the pond. She didn't scold them when they came out. She looked at their spoon-shaped beaks, and at their webbed feet, and knew that they were ducklings.

"What a mistake I made!" she said. "I brought them up to be good chicks – but they will all grow into ducks!"

He Didn't Want a Bath

"TINKER! Tinker! Where are you?" called Margery. "I want to give you a bath."

Tinker knew that quite well. As soon as he had seen the big wooden tub out on the grass he knew that he was to have that horrid thing, a bath!

Tinker hated baths. He hated having to stand in lukewarm water and be rubbed with soap and then scrubbed with a brush. He couldn't bear feeling himself wet and clean all over.

So he was lying under the bushes, very quietly indeed, hoping that Margery wouldn't see him.

"Tony – where's that dog gone?" called Margery to her brother. "He *always* disappears at bath-time, always. He's really very annoying. I have everything ready, and the water's in the bath – but there's no dog."

"There he is, under the bushes," said Tony, pointing. "I can see the end of his tail. He always forgets his tail when he hides!"

Margery saw the end of Tinker's tail. She

crept up to it. She pounced – and Tinker sprang up. But it was too late. Margery had him by the collar now and was marching him to the bath.

Tinker whined. Margery had to get Tony to hold him in the water for her, because he struggled so. She soaped him well, and he wriggled about till some went in his eyes. Then he howled dismally. Margery squeezed clear water over his head to get the soap out of his eyes.

He really was very naughty. He tried to jump out of the bath. He stood on the soap and went sideways into the soapy water with such a splash that he soaked Margery and Tony from head to foot.

Margery slapped him. "Tinker! You are being very, very silly. Look what you've done! Now stand still while I scrub you."

He didn't stand still. He screwed this way and that way, and almost pulled Tony into the bath with him. And when at last he was rinsed and out on the grass, he shook himself so violently that hundreds of silvery drops flew all over Margery and Tony, and even over Granny, who was sitting quite a long way off!

"Really! Tinker can be very naughty," she said, wiping her skirt.

"Yes, he can. Tony, hold him while I try to dry him," said poor Margery – but, dear me, Tinker was off and away over the grass. *He* wasn't going to be dried! He was going to have a very good time indeed, now. He sniffed at himself. How horrid he smelt – all that nasty soap. What would the other dogs think when he met them?

They didn't like his smell at all. When he trotted up to Laddie, Laddie smelt him all over and then turned away in disgust.

"You don't smell like a *dog*," he said, "You smell disgusting. Go and roll in something nice and get that smell off!"

Tinker went to the field. He squeezed under

the gate. There was a muddy patch by the stream where the cows stood. It always smelt very strong indeed. He would roll in that and then he would smell much better.

So he rolled in the mud, over and over. He looked very peculiar when he had finished. He was covered in patches of brown mud that smelt very strong.

He shook himself and went back to Laddie. "Do I smell better now?" he said.

"A bit," said Laddie. "But I can still smell that soap. Look – rub yourself against that fence over there. It smells very strong indeed, but I don't know what of."

A man had been painting the fence bright green and the paint was still wet. Tinker rubbed himself against it, first one side and then the other. Then he put his head over his shoulder and stared at himself doubtfully. He thought he looked a bit strange, with mud and now green paint. Also, he didn't like the smell of the paint after all. It made him feel sick.

Laddie didn't like it either. He sniffed at Tinker once more, looked disgusted and put his nose in the air. "Horrible!" he said. "Go and swim in the duck-pond, for goodness' sake, Tinker, and get that green stuff off!" Poor

Tinker. He flung himself in the duck-pond and swam there. He got tangled in the weeds and came out with them twined round his head and legs. They smelt rather strong, too. But Laddie liked that smell better.

"That green stuff hasn't come off you," he said, "and I can still smell a bit of soap. But you do smell better now. I'll have a game."

So they had a game, and by the time they had finished, Tinker's coat was dry – but, dear me, the patches of brown mud and the green paint made him look very strange – and the pond-water had left a very strong smell indeed.

"It's time to go home," said Laddie. "Goodbye."

He went off to his home and Tinker trotted away to his. He went in at the front door and into the house. He was tired. He jumped up on to the sofa and lay down on the cushions there.

Mother found him. She tracked him by the terrible smell! She gave a shriek when she saw him. "*Tinker!* What *have* you been doing, you dreadful dog? You smell simply *frightful!* Margery! Tony! Come and take Tinker out of here at once. He needs a bath."

Margery and Tony came running. "Oh, you

bad dog! Mother, he's just *had* a bath! Oh, you bad, naughty dog!"

They hauled him off. Margery went to get the tub. Tony went to get the water. Tinker went to hide in the bushes – and as usual he left his tail out.

And curiously enough, this story is going to end *exactly* as it began, which stories hardly ever do.

"Tinker! Tinker! Where are you?" called Margery. "I want to give you a bath!"

Stones For A Donkey

"HEY, Tom, go and fetch my donkey and take him up the hill to Mrs. Brown's," shouted the farmer. "She has got some washing to send back to my wife, and the donkey can bring it."

"Right, sir," said Tom, and went to fetch the little grey donkey. He was a fat little animal, good-natured and strong. Tom soon got him out of the field, jumped on his back and rode him away.

Now, it was winter-time. The roads had frozen in the night, and they were very slippery indeed. It was all right for the donkey so long as he was on the level road, but as soon as he began to climb the hill, his hooves began to slip.

"Come on, now, come on!" said Tom, who was an impatient boy. "Get along there!"

The donkey tried again, but his feet slipped badly, and he was afraid of falling over. So he stood still.

Tom hit him with a stick. "Will you get on, stupid creature? How am I to get to the top of the hill and back if you stand still like this?"

The donkey would not move. Tom got off and tried to push him up the hill. But the donkey wouldn't budge. He wasn't going to fall down and break his leg if he could help it!

By the side of the road there were heaps of small stones. Tom felt cross, and he went to the stones. He picked up a handful and threw them hard at the donkey. They hit him on his back and made him jump. He started forward a step or two.

"Ha! That makes you move!" cried Tom, pleased. He picked up another handful of the stones and flung them with all his might. The poor little donkey was hurt in a dozen places, and brayed loudly.

"Move on, I tell you, move on!" shouted Tom, but the donkey would not go for more than one or two steps. So Tom threw more and more stones at him, getting angrier and angrier.

A smaller boy came up the hill and looked at Tom. "Those stones are hurting the donkey," he said. "Do stop throwing them at the poor thing. Can't you see he is afraid of moving on because his feet slip?"

"Oh, he's just stupid, that's all," said Tom.

"And don't you interfere with me, or I'll throw stones at you too!"

"Shall I help you?" said the boy, not taking any notice of Tom's angry voice.

"How can you help me?" said Tom roughly. "It's only these stones that will get the donkey to move."

"Yes, you're right," said the boy. "But I could use the stones in quite a different way to make him move. Shall I show you?"

Tom nodded. He felt sure that no way of using the stones would make the donkey move on, except the way he himself had used –throwing a handful as hard as he could.

"I live just here," said the boy, pointing to a house. "I won't be a minute. I'm going to get something."

He ran to a shed beside the house and came out with a small spade. Tom was surprised. What did he want a spade for?

The boy began to dig into the heaps of small stones by the roadside, and he spread them in front of the donkey, making a path of stones for him to walk on.

"You see, the road here is terribly slippery," explained the boy in his gentle voice. "Horses donkeys are always falling down on this steep bit, and breaking their legs. So these heaps of small pebbles are placed here for people to scatter in front of their animals."

"Oh," said Tom, suddenly feeling stupid and small.

"It's no good expecting an animal to go on if it cannot get a firm hold with its feet," said the boy, busy shovelling hard. "Better to help it, than to hinder it, don't you think so?"

"Yes," said Tom.

"Now," said the boy, "we'll see what the donkey says about things this time. Come along, old fellow. Walk on the stones, and you'll be all right."

The donkey put out a foot and felt the stones, which gave him a good grip on the slippery road. He walked a few steps over the scattered pebbles, and went safely up the very steep part of the road.

"There you are!" said the boy. "Now he'll be all right, I think. Anyway, there are little heaps of pebbles beside any very steep bit, so you'll know what to do another time."

"Thanks," said Tom, and went on up the hill with the donkey. He thought hard. He had been stupid, but that boy had been clever. He had been unkind, but that boy had taken pity on the donkey. He had tried to force the donkey on by cruelty, but that boy had helped it on with kindness.

"I don't think much of myself," thought Tom, ashamed. "Poor little donkey!"

"Hee-haw!" said the donkey, looking round at Tom. "Hee-haw! There are two ways of using stones! Just remember that, Tom! And there are two ways of doing anything, the good way and the bad way. Hee-haw!"

The Careless Kitten

THERE was once a madcap of a kitten. This little kitten just simply didn't care what silly and dangerous thing she did. She leapt here and she leapt there. She ran up the curtains. She hid under the bed. She got between people's feet and tripped them over and almost got stepped on herself!

The kitten's mother lived at the house next door and was always hearing tales of this madcap kitten of hers.

"Do you know, that kitten of yours jumped into the pond today!" cried the big dog. "Splash it went! It was after the goldfish, silly little thing! It was a good thing my mistress was there to rescue her. She might have drowned!"

"And will you believe it, she scratched the big dog up the road," chirped a sparrow who lived in the garden. "*Scratched* it! Well, if the kitten hadn't leapt up a tree at once it would have been badly bitten! She won't live very long if she carries on like this!"

The kitten's mother was very worried. She

111

spoke to the dog who lived with the same family as the kitten. "That's twice my kitten has lost one of her lives," she said. "Twice! She only has seven lives left to lose, now, and she is hardly four months old."

"Seven lives left – what do you mean?" said the dog, looking very puzzled.

"Well, didn't you know that all cats have nine lives?" said the cat. "I suppose you poor dogs only have one. Well, we have nine – and I'm so afraid my kitten is using hers up too quickly. Once nearly drowned – once nearly bitten by a dog – that's two lives gone in a week."

"I'll warn her," the dog promised the kitten's worried mother. But before he had a chance to speak to the kitten, she climbed up to the roof of the house and fell off it right down to the ground. The dog ran up to see if she was still alive – and suddenly she leapt up and ran off, laughing at the dog.

"That's three lives gone!" called the dog. "Come here! I want to talk to you."

But the kitten was busy thinking about what to play next and didn't hear him. She ran off.

The dog watched for her, and saw her in the outside the house the very next day. He ran to tell her what her mother had said – but before he could reach her, the little thing ran straight across to the other side of the road. A car came along at the same moment and the kitten disappeared under it.

"Well – it will be killed this time for certain," thought the dog sadly. "Her mother will be so upset." But no, the kitten came out from under the car as frisky as ever. Not one of the wheels had touched it. The dog couldn't believe his eyes.

"Hey! That's four lives gone!" barked the dog. "Will you please come here, you silly thing! I've a message from your mother."

"I don't want to hear it," mewed the kitten. "Mother's always scolding me. Go away."

She ran up a tree and the dog couldn't get near her. He stood and barked at the bottom. The kitten ran down, patted him on the nose and ran off in front of him. He ran after her, determined to make her listen. But she ran straight up a tall flag-pole to the very, very top!

And, of course, she couldn't get down. When she tried to she lost her balance and fell – right on top of the surprised dog! Luckily, neither of them was hurt. He tried to grab her in his mouth, but she was off again at once. "Listen!

That's *five* lives gone!" barked the dog anxiously. "Do, do listen to me."

But the kitten wouldn't. She ran into the house and the dog couldn't follow. He had to stay in his kennel out in the garden and wasn't allowed inside the house.

A week later he saw the kitten again. She was prancing about round a horse's hooves. The horse belonged to a rag-and-bone man who had stopped outside the house. Down came a hoof on the kitten's tail – just missing the little thing's head.

"Another life gone," groaned the dog. "Only

three more left. She'll have lost them all before I can warn her about them."

Then the kitten lost two more lives very quickly indeed. She jumped up on a wobbly pile of heavy books, and they toppled over and fell on top of her – almost crushing the life out of her tiny body – and in a great fright she rushed up to the bathroom to where Sammy, the little boy, was having a bath, and jumped straight into the water to be with him! Luckily, Mummy was there to rescue her.

She carried the kitten downstairs to dry in the sun. She was wet through and very frightened. Mother put her down by the big dog.

"Look after the poor little thing for me," she said. "She's nearly killed herself by overbalancing a great pile of books and then by leaping into Sammy's bath-water. Get a little sense into her head, Rover."

"Eight lives lost," said the big dog, and he licked the kitten gently. She was very, very wet.

"What's all this you keep saying about lives being lost?" she said.

So Rover told her. "You have nine lives, like any cat – and you're throwing them all away, one by one. You've lost eight of your lives already. You only have one left to last you now. What are you going to do about it?"

"Good gracious – why didn't someone tell me this before!" said the kitten in alarm. "I shall be very, very careful now. I shall lose my silly ways and grow into a sensible, well-behaved cat."

So she did – and everyone said, "Oh, what a pity it is that kittens so soon grow up and lose their playful ways and turn into solemn sedate cats."

Well, now you know why they do – it's because somebody suddenly tells them about their nine lives, and they decide not to waste any more! How many lives has *your* cat had? Mine's had about seven already.

Mike's Monkey

WHEN Mike's birthday came his uncle Ned gave him a strange present. It was a little brown monkey!

"Here you are!" said Uncle Ned, and he put the monkey into Mike's arms. "Here's a little monkey for you. He's quite young, so you can teach him anything. He'll copy everything you do and give you a lot of fun."

"Well," said Mother, "I hope he treats his monkey better than he treats his toys. He is always breaking those. And he hardly has a book left, he tears the pages so."

It was quite true. Mike did spoil his things dreadfully. He broke so many, he left his toys out in the rain, he spoilt his books, and broke all his chalks.

"You destroy all your nice things," his mother said to him. "You really must get out of the habit. Look at that nice teddy bear you had – you've pulled out all his whiskers and cut off his ears. That's very naughty of you."

Anyway, Mike couldn't do that kind of thing

to a live monkey. And he didn't want to, for he loved the little thing. It slept in Mike's wheelbarrow, covered by a little rug. It ate fruit, and loved a bit of cucumber. It had the funniest ways, and Mike loved it very much.

It went with him everywhere, sitting on his shoulder. It copied everything he did. It even learnt to hold a cup by the handle and drink from it.

It copied Mike when he cleaned his teeth. It copied him when he brushed his hair – except that the monkey brushed its nose instead of its hair!

One day Mike was in the nursery, playing with his toys. He was in one of his naughty moods. He broke his little sailor doll. He broke his engine. He tore a whole page out of a book. He took a pencil and scribbled all over the door of the toy cupboard.

The monkey watched him. It liked to do everything that Mike did. It took a flower vase off the mantelpiece and threw it on the floor, where it broke.

Then it threw down the clock. Mike was full of horror. Whatever would Mother say! The monkey took some books from the bookcases and began to tear pages out of them, just as it had seen Mike do. When Mike tried to stop it, it leapt to the top of the curtain, where Mike couldn't reach it, and went on tearing out pages.

Then it leapt down, took Mike's pencil and began to scribble all over the walls of the room. Mike knew his mother would be very angry indeed.

So she was. When she came in, she glared at Mike and said, "So you are in one of your naughty moods! Look at my clock, and my vase! Look at those books, all torn! And just see this dreadful scribbling all over the walls!"

"Mother – the monkey did it," said Mike, afraid that he was going to get a beating.

"Then if that is so, the monkey will have to go," said Mother at once. "I'm not going to have everything destroyed like this. What a naughty little creature!"

"Oh, Mother – it wasn't really the monkey's fault," said Mike. "It was mine. I was naughty first. I broke Sailor Doll, and my engine, and I tore a book. And I scribbled over the toy cupboard door."

"I see," said Mother. "Well – I will forgive the monkey this time. As for you, you will go to bed for the rest of the day."

The next morning was fine, so Mike and the monkey went out of doors. Mike had a horrid way of knocking the heads off the daisies with a stick – he did so like spoiling things, which was a very bad habit. He picked up a stick and began to swish the heads off all the flowers in the grass.

The monkey thought that was a good idea. It took up a stick too, and went to a bed of flowers. Soon it was knocking all the heads off, and the gardener came rushing up in a rage.

"Look at that! I'll tell your mother! I won't have a monkey like that in the garden if it's going to spoil all my work. I'll tell your mother."

He did – and Mother said that settled it, the monkey had to go.

Mike wept and wailed. He loved his monkey. It wouldn't be happy without him. He wanted it so badly. It might die if it hadn't got him to look after it.

"Now look here, Mike," said his mother, "it's no good making all this fuss. It's all your own fault and you know it. You have this bad habit of breaking and spoiling things for no reason at all, and the monkey copies you in everything. Whenever you spoil things, as you so often do, the monkey is going to spoil things too, so there will be two stupid people instead of one."

"I didn't know I was so bad about spoiling things," wept Mike. "I just did it without thinking. Now I see my monkey doing it too, I do see how horrid it is. Give the monkey another chance, Mother, please do. I love him so."

Mother didn't say anything for a minute. Then she spoke more gently. "I'll give *you* another chance, Mike, and see if you really do want to keep the monkey, and love him as much as you say you do. It rests with you whether you keep him or not. Get out of this silly habit of spoiling things, and the monkey will no longer copy you in that, and he can stay."

"Oh, I will, I will!" said Mike, drying his eyes.

"But if you break or tear or spoil anything again for no reason at all, and the monkey does the same, he will have to go," said Mother. "Now we will see if you love him enough to behave yourself."

Mike took the tiny monkey into his arms. The little creature nestled there, looking up at him with bright eyes, for it loved Mike.

"I didn't know how silly I was to destroy things till you showed me, Monkey," said Mike. "Don't you get into bad habits like I have. Get into good ones! I'll try and get good ones too, and then you can copy them."

That was a week ago. You will be glad to know that the monkey is still with Mike. I do hope Mike will be able to keep the little thing, don't you?

He's a Horrid Dog

"THERE'S a dear little puppy next door," said Mummy to Alice. "I saw him this morning. You'll love him, Alice."

"I'll look out for him as I go to school," said Alice. So she did, and she soon saw him, running round the next-door garden. The gate was shut, so he couldn't get out. Alice peeped over the top, and he rushed up and licked her on the nose.

"Don't," said Alice, who didn't know that licking was a dog's way of kissing. She went off down the street, her satchel over her back, and her ball in her hand. She was not allowed to bounce it in the road, in case it went too near cars and she ran after it. She wanted to play with it at break.

Suddenly there came the sound of scampering feet, and after her tore the puppy! He had managed to jump over the gate, and wanted to catch her up. He had smelt the ball in her hand.

A ball. How that puppy loved a ball! His mistress often threw one for him, and he loved to scamper after it and get it into his mouth. A ball was the greatest fun in the world!

He jumped up at the surprised little girl. He knocked the ball right out of her hand! It went rolling along the pavement, and Alice gave a cry of alarm.

"Naughty dog! You'll make me lose my ball!"

The puppy pounced on it, threw it into the air, caught it again, and then danced all round Alice as if to say, "Catch me if you can! I have your ball!"

But he wouldn't let Alice catch him, or get her ball, either. He ran off as soon as she tried to grab him. "You're a horrid, horrid dog!" said Alice, almost in tears. "I don't like you a bit. Give me my ball! You'll make me late for school."

But the puppy was having such a lovely game that he couldn't possibly let Alice catch him. So, in the end, she had to go to school without her ball. She was late and the teacher scolded her.

"It wasn't my fault," said Alice. "It was the fault of the dog next door. He's a horrid dog. He took my ball away from me and wouldn't give it back."

The puppy was waiting for her to come home, and as soon as he saw her he rushed out and put the ball at her feet. Really, he wanted her to play with him, and throw the ball for him to fetch. Alice wasn't doing that!

She picked up her ball and looked at it. The puppy had chewed it a little, and it wasn't such a nice-looking ball as before. Alice was very cross. She stamped her foot at the puppy and made him jump. "Bad dog! Horrid dog! I don't like you! Go home!"

"Why, Alice!" said her mother's voice in surprise. "I thought you'd love the puppy!"

"I don't. He's a horrid dog! I shan't play with him or take any notice of him at all," said Alice. "He's unkind and mean."

And, do you know, she wouldn't pat him or talk to him, no matter how often he came rushing up to her. He was surprised and sad. Usually everyone made a fuss of him, for he really was a dear little fellow, with a tail that never stopped wagging.

Now, one afternoon Alice was going out to tea. She put on her best blue frock, socks and shoes, and a new hat with a blue ribbon round. It suited Alice beautifully.

"That's the prettiest hat you've ever had,"

said Mummy, and kissed her goodbye. "Hold it on tightly round the corner, because it's very windy today."

Alice set off. The puppy came to meet her as usual, and as usual she took no notice of him at all. He trotted behind her, his tail down. What a funny little girl this was! Why didn't she give him a pat? The puppy couldn't understand it at all.

At the corner the wind blew very hard. Off went Alice's beautiful new hat. It flew into the road and rolled over and over and over, all the way back home. Alice gave a real squeal. "Oh! My new hat! Oh, dear!"

The puppy saw the hat rolling gaily along and he tore after it, barking. Was this a new game? Had the little girl thrown her hat for him to play with?

He was almost run over by a car. Then a bicycle just missed him. The hat rolled in and out of the traffic, and the puppy scampered after it. He caught the hat at last and was just going to toss it into the air and catch it again when he heard Alice's voice, "Bring it here! Puppy, bring it here! It's my best hat!"

Ah! He knew the words "bring it here!" He tore back to Alice at once and dropped the hat at her feet, his tail wagging hard. He looked up at the little girl with shining eyes and his pink tongue hung out of his mouth.

Alice picked up the hat. It wasn't hurt at all. She dusted it a little, and then put it on. She looked down at the puppy. "Thank you," she said. "That was kind of you, especially as we weren't friends. But we will be now!"

"Woof!" said the puppy, and to Alice's surprise he put out his paw. Did he want to shake hands? He did! This was his newest trick and he was proud of it. Alice felt sure he was trying to say, "Yes, we'll be friends! Shake hands!"

So they shook hands solemnly, and the puppy went all the way to her aunt's with Alice, waited for her, and then went all the way home. And she asked him in to play with her in her garden.

"But I thought you said he was a horrid dog?" said Mummy, in surprise.

"I made a mistake," said Alice. "*I* was the horrid one, Mummy – but now we're *both* nice!"

Woffly the Rabbit and Quick-Ears the Hare

ONCE there was a young rabbit called Woffly. He lived in a burrow with his family, and he was very happy.

"It's fun to be a rabbit!" said Woffly. "It's fun to go out in the evening and nibble the nice juicy grass. It's fun to chase the other rabbits and fun to play hide-and-seek in the burrows."

One day Woffly ran down the hillside far away from the others. He had always been told not to do this, but he did so badly want to know what was at the bottom of the hill.

There was a field there. Woffly ran out on to it – and suddenly he met somebody rather like himself. The two animals stared at one another.

"Hallo," said Woffly at last. "Are you a rabbit?"

"No, I'm a hare," said the little creature. "I'm not very old. My name is Quick-Ears. I hear very, very well, you know."

"You are very like me," said Woffly. "You must be a cousin of mine."

"I am," said Quick-Ears. "And that is why

we are rather alike. But you are smaller than I am, and your ears are not so long. Your eyes are smaller than mine too."

"You have black tips to your ears, and I haven't," said Woffly. "Shall we have a race? I am sure I can run faster than you!"

"Of course you can't!" said the little hare. "Hares can always run faster than rabbits. Now then – one, two, three – go!"

Off they went across the field. But Quick-Ears was right. He was the faster of the two, and he won quite easily.

"Stay with me for a little while," he said to Woffly. "I like you. Play with me for a few days."

"Where is your hole?" asked Woffly. "I like to be near a hole so that I can pop down if danger comes."

"Don't be silly!" said Quick-Ears. "A hole indeed! No hare needs a hole to hide in! He can always get away on his quick legs. His ears and eyes and nose tell him when enemies are near, and he can run faster than any of them!"

"Well, where is your home, then, if you haven't a hole?" said Woffly in wonder.

"I'll show you," said the hare, and he took Woffly to the middle of the field. He showed him a dent in the dry ground there. "This is my home," he said. "I just settle down into this dent I have made with my body – and there I sleep and rest."

"I want a rest now," said Woffly. "I am tired after our race. Shall we lie down side by side and rest?"

"You can have my place," said the hare. "I will make myself another beside you."

Woffly settled down into the hare's place, and Quick-Ears made himself another beside him, moving his body about in the earth until he had made himself a good resting-place his own size and shape.

"I must go to sleep," said Woffly, closing his eyes. "That was a long race."

He slept – and so did Quick-Ears. But after a while the ever-ready ears of the little hare heard a sound, even though he was asleep. His big eyes flicked open, and his nose quivered. His ears heard the slightest sound across the fields. He heard the high squeak of the flying bat, the tiny squeal of a far-away mouse, the brush of the owl's wings as it flew.

The sound came again, and Quick-Ears knew what it was. The red fox!

He leapt up and awoke Woffly. "Run! Run!

The red fox is coming! Run!"

Poor Woffly. He looked about for a hole to dart into, but there was none. There was only the open field around him. He ran off, right across it, his little white bobtail showing behind him.

Quick-Ears went with him. When they came to the hillside, the little hare stopped and listened, his big ears sticking straight up from his head.

"He's coming this way!" he said suddenly. "I heard the click of his claws against a stone. Up the hillside, quickly, rabbit, or the red fox will catch us!"

"Here's my burrow! Here's my burrow!" panted Woffly. "Follow me! Follow my white bobbing tail, Quick-Ears. I will take you to safety! No fox can get down my burrow!"

He darted into a hole, his white bobtail showing clearly, a guide to the running hare behind. Both animals lay down at the bottom of the burrow, panting.

"You must stay a day or two with me," said the rabbit. "You cannot go out if the red fox is about. He eats hares and rabbits, even big ones."

"Yes, I will stay with you," said the hare.

"Perhaps a hole is better to hide in, after all."

"Don't keep putting your ears up," said Woffly. "Put them down flat – like this."

He showed Quick-Ears how to lay his ears flat – but the little hare kept forgetting.

"I can't hear properly with my ears laid flat," he grumbled. "I simply can't hear!"

"You don't need to, when you are safe in a hole," said Woffly. "There is no danger about in our burrows. We are safe here. Do keep your ears down, Quick-Ears."

The little hare tried his hardest to keep his ears flat, but whenever he heard a noise, his ears flicked themselves upright. Soon they became quite bruised against the roof of the burrow.

"I want to go out of this hole," said the little hare, the next morning. "I want to put my ears up for a while. They don't like always being flat. Let's go out and play. We can keep near the burrow, in case the red fox comes along."

So out they went on to the dewy hillside. The grass was short and sweet. There were many rabbits playing together. It was fun.

"I can see how useful your white bobtails are, when so many of you play together," said Quick-Ears. "When a rabbit sees danger, he turns to run to his hole – and his white bobtail flashes up and down, so that all the other rabbits suddenly catch sight of it – and they run too."

"Yes, it's a good idea," said Woffly. "And there's another good idea we have too. When a rabbit smells danger and wants to warn everyone on the hillside, he drums with his hind legs on the ground. We all hear the noise, and we run for our lives!"

The little hare liked playing with the rabbits. He ran races with them, but he always won. Woffly told the others how hard Quick-Ears found it to keep his ears flat when he was under the ground.

That made them laugh. "Oh, all rabbits hold

their ears flat, when they are in their burrows," said a small rabbit. "Fancy you not knowing how to do it, hare!"

"I do know how to do it," said Quick-Ears, "but after all, I am not used to burrows, as you are. You would not like lying out in the open under the stars, if you came to stay with me. We all have our own ways."

A curious sound came up the hillside. R-r-r-r-r-r-r! R-r-r-r-r-r-r! All the rabbits stopped feeding and looked up, their ears upright.

"That's old Whiskers drumming with his hind legs to say danger is about!" said Woffly. "I expect it's the red fox again. Quick, we must go!"

All the rabbits were rushing off to their holes, their white bobtails showing clearly. Quick-Ears did not follow Woffly. Instead he raced off down the hill.

Woffly called after him.

"Quick-Ears! Quick-Ears! Come back! It is not safe down there. Come into my burrow and hide. You will be quite safe there."

"No, no, Woffly!" cried the little hare. "I do not feel safe in your narrow, dark burrow! I want the light and the open air! I want the sun above me, and the stars at night. I would rather trust to my quick ears and swift legs, than to your dark burrow!"

"Let him go," said old Whiskers. "Hares and rabbits are different, with their own ways and their own likings. Let him go!"

So Woffly ran to his hole, and Quick-Ears ran to his field. Hares will be hares and rabbits will be rabbits!

The two often meet and play a game together – but each thinks his own way of life is best. And so it is, for him!

The Dog Who Wanted a Home

THERE was once a dog who wanted a home. He had had a bad master, who whipped him every day, and he had run away because he was so unhappy.

"I shall find a new master, or perhaps a mistress," said the dog to himself. "I want someone who will love me. I want someone to love and to care for."

But nobody seemed to want a dog, nobody at all. It was very sad. The dog ran here and he ran there, but either there was already a dog in the houses he went to, or the people there didn't want a dog.

He talked to his friend, the cat, about it. "What am I to do?" he said. "I must have a home. I cannot run about wild, with no food, and only the puddles to drink from."

"Dogs and cats need homes," said the cat, licking herself as she sat on top of the wall. "I don't know of anyone who wants a dog. It's a pity you are not a cat."

"Why?" asked the dog.

"Because I know a poor, blind old lady who badly wants a cat," said the cat. "She is lonely, and she wants a nice, cosy cat she can have in her lap."

"Perhaps she would have a dog instead," said the dog. "If she is blind, I could help her, couldn't I? I could take her safely across the roads, and guard her house at night. A cat couldn't do that."

"Well, she says she wants a cat, not a dog," said the cat. Then she stopped licking herself and looked closely at the dog.

"I have an idea!" she said. "You have a very silky coat for a dog, and a very long tail. I wonder whether you could *pretend* to be a cat! The poor old lady is blind and she wouldn't know."

"I shouldn't like to deceive anyone," said the dog.

"No, that wouldn't be nice," said the cat. "But after all, a dog *would* be better for the old lady, and when she got used to you, you could tell her you were a dog, and ask her to forgive you for pretending."

"And by that time she might be so fond of me that she wouldn't mind keeping me!" said the dog joyfully. "Yes – that is quite a good idea of yours, cat."

"I will give you a few hints about cats," said the cat. "Don't bark, whatever you do, because, as you know, cats mew. If you bark you will give yourself away. And do try and purr a little."

The dog tried – but what came from his throat was more of a growl than a purr. The cat laughed.

"That's really enough to make a cat laugh!" she said. "Well, perhaps with a little practice you may get better. And another thing to remember is – put your claws in when you walk, so that you walk softly, like me, and don't make a clattering sound."

The dog looked at his paws. The big, blunt claws stuck out, and he could not move them back into his paws, as the cat could. "I must try to practice that too," he said.

"Good-bye," said the cat. "I wish you luck. She is a dear old lady and will be very kind to you."

The dog ran off to the old lady's house. She was sitting in her kitchen, knitting. The dog ran up to her, and pressed against her, as he had seen cats do. The old lady put down her hand and stroked him.

"So someone has sent me a cat!" she said. "How kind! Puss, puss, puss, do you want some milk?"

She got up and put down a saucer of milk. The dog was pleased. He lapped it up noisily.

"Dear me, what a noise you make!" said the old lady in surprise. "You must be a very hungry cat! Come on to my knee."

The dog jumped up on to the old lady's knee. She stroked his silky coat, and felt his long tail. He tried his very best to purr. He made a very funny noise.

"You must have got a cold, Puss," said the old lady. "That's a funny purr you have! Now, go to sleep."

The dog fell asleep. He liked being in the old lady's warm lap. He felt loved and happy. If only she went on thinking that he was a cat.

When he woke up, the old lady spoke to him. "Puss, I want you to lie in the kitchen to-night and catch the mice that come. You will be very useful to me if you can do that."

The dog was not good at catching mice. He was not quiet and sly like the cat. But he made up his mind to try. He did try, very hard, but as soon as he jumped up when he saw a mouse, the little animal heard his claws clattering on the floor, and fled away.

So in the morning there were no dead mice for the old lady to find. She was quite nice about it and stroked the dog gently.

"Never mind, Puss," she said. "You can try again to-night."

The old lady was so kind and gentle that the dog longed with all his heart to catch mice for her, or to do anything to please her. He trotted after her all day long, as she went about her work. It was wonderful what she could do without being able to see.

"The only thing I can't do with safety is to go out and see my grand-children," she told the dog. "You see, I have to cross two roads to get to their house, and I am always afraid of being knocked over by something I can't see."

The dog nearly said, "Woof, woof, I will help you," and just remembered in time that cats never bark.

The old lady was puzzled that day. Every time the dog ran across the floor she put her head on one side and listened.

"Your paws make such a noise," she said. "Surely you put your sharp claws in as you run, Puss? It sounds as if you are making quite a noise with them."

So the dog was, because he couldn't help it. He couldn't put his claws in, like a cat. No dog can.

Then another thing puzzled the old lady. She put some milk on her finger for the dog to lick. The dog put out his pink tongue and licked the milk away.

"Well!" said the old lady, surprised. "What a strange tongue you have, Puss! All the other cats I have had had very rough, scraping tongues – but you have a very smooth one!"

"Oh dear!" thought the dog. "This is quite true. Dogs have smooth tongues, and cats have rough ones. I remember an old cat licking me once, and I noticed how rough her tongue was – almost as if it was covered by tiny hooks!"

"I'll give you a nice meaty bone, Puss," said the old lady at tea-time. "You can scrape the meat off it with your tongue, and when you have taken away the meat, we will give the bone to the next-door dog to crunch. Cats cannot crunch bones, but dogs can!"

The dog was delighted to see the lovely, meaty bone. He lay down and began to lick it with his tongue, as cats do. But his tongue was not rough, and he could not get the meat off the bone.

It was sad. He was hungry and longed to crunch up the bone. He sniffed at it. He licked it again. Then he got it into his mouth and gave it a bite with his hard, strong dog's teeth, that were so different from the teeth of cats!

The bone made a noise as he crunched it up. The old lady was surprised. "Well, I never heard a cat crunch up a big bone before!" she said. "You must have strong teeth, Puss!"

She put on her hat and coat. "I am going out," she said. "I shall try to get to the house where my grand-children live. Maybe someone will help me across the road. Keep house for me whilst I am gone, Puss."

The dog did not like to see the blind old lady going out alone. He ran after her. When she came to the road she had to cross, he stood in front of her, making her wait until a bicycle had gone by. Then he gently tugged at her dress to show her that it was safe to go across.

The old lady was delighted. She bent down to stroke the dog. "Puss, you are the cleverest cat in the world!" she said.

But dear me, when the old lady reached her grand-children safely, what a surprise for her! They ran out to greet her, all shouting the same thing.

"Granny! You've got a dog! Oh, what a nice one!"

And so at last the secret was out. "No wonder I was so puzzled!" said the old lady, stooping to pat the dog. He barked a little, and licked her hand, wagging his tail hard.

"That's right!" said the old lady. "Don't pretend to be a cat any more! Bark, and lick my hand and wag your tail! I'll have you instead of a cat. You're a kind little animal, and you'll help me across the road, won't you?"

"Woof, woof, woof!" said the dog joyfully, and ran off to tell the cat that he had found a home at last.

The Runaway Cows

TOM, Dick, Harry and Will were coming home from school one day, when they saw five red and white cows walking down the road.

"Look at those cows!" said Tom. "All by themselves! They must have got out of the field and run away."

"They belong to Farmer White," said Dick. "Won't he be wild?"

"We'd better tell him," said Harry.

"No, we won't," said Will. "He's a horrid man. He shouts at boys and girls. And you know he won't let anyone go blackberrying in that field where the hedges are simply covered with big blackberries."

"So we won't bother about his old cows," said Tom. "We'll let them run right away, and perhaps be knocked down by cars."

"That's not right," said Dick at once. "Why should we let the cows come to harm just because we don't like the farmer? You're always saying things like that, Tom."

"Well, anyway, why should we bother?" said

Will lazily. "It's not our business. They're not our cows. Nobody can make us go and tell the farmer they are loose."

"That's just it," said Harry. "Nobody can make us – it isn't our business – but if *some*body doesn't take some trouble about those cows, they'll be hurt. We ought to make it our job to see they aren't."

"Well, all I say is, I hope that horrid farmer's cows do get hurt," said Tom, who was spiteful. "I'm going home."

"And I jolly well won't bother myself to go out of my way to tell the farmer," said Will. "I want my tea." So he went home with Tom. Dick and Harry looked at one another. They were both sensible boys who liked animals and would not let them get hurt if they could help it.

"It's true we don't like Farmer White," said Harry, "but all the same we ought to go and tell him. I'll go, Dick, and you chase after the cows and try and head them back."

So Dick chased after the cows and managed to turn them back up the road again, whilst Harry went to tell the farmer.

He was having his tea. "What's up?" he said, when he saw Harry.

"Five of your cows are loose on the road, sir," said Harry. "I've sent Dick to turn them back, but perhaps you had better come and take them to their field. Dick isn't very used to cows."

"Thanks," said the farmer, getting up. "It's nice to see a boy who'll take the trouble to put things right without being asked to! I'll come now."

They went out and soon met Dick with the cows. He had found a stick and was feeling quite important chasing the cows back to the farm.

"Good of you to trouble," said the farmer. "I must find out who left my gate open. Just go ahead and see if it's shut or open now, will you?"

It was open. "There you are!" said the farmer crossly. "Some silly boy left it open, I suppose, in spite of the notice on it, PLEASE SHUT THIS GATE. Well – I should think all boys were silly and tiresome if you hadn't given me your help today. Thank you."

"Very pleased to help you," said Dick politely. Just as they were going, the farmer turned back and shouted.

"Hi! Do you like blackberries?"

"Oh yes!" said both the boys.

"Well, there are some fine ones on the hedge in that field over there," said the farmer, pointing with his finger. "You and your friend can go and pick them whenever you like. I won't let other boys into the field because they leave the gates open."

"Oh, *thanks*!" said Dick and Harry in delight. Goodness – they would be able to take big baskets home full of ripe blackberries tomorrow.

"What a bit of luck!" said Harry, as they went home. "Weren't Tom and Will silly not to come and help with the cows too?"

The next day the two boys went to get the blackberries. They filled two big baskets and took them home. On the way back they met Tom and Will. How the boys stared when they saw the enormous blackberries.

"We got them in the field over there," said Dick, pointing.

"You're not allowed to go there," said Will at once.

"Yes, we are. The farmer said we could," said Dick, and told Will and Tom all that had happened the day before.

"You might take us with you tomorrow,"

said Tom. Harry shook his head.

"No," he said. "You wouldn't help yesterday, Tom, and we did. We didn't expect a reward, of course, but it was nice to get one. If you'd helped, you would have shared. As it is, the farmer said that only Dick and I were to go."

"Well, I shall help next time!" said Tom, looking ashamed. "I'm glad the cows weren't hurt. You deserve the blackberries, Harry!"

How they enjoyed the blackberry tarts their mothers made – but they did deserve a treat didn't they?

Old Ugly, the Water-Grub

ONCE upon a time there was an ugly grub that lived in a little pond.

At first it was only small, but as time went on it grew. It had a long body, with many joints, and six legs on which it could crawl about in the mud.

The other creatures in the pond thought it was very ugly indeed. "Look at it!" said the pretty little stickleback. "I'd be ashamed of myself if I was as ugly as that!"

"I don't like its face," said a water-snail with a nicely-curved shell. "There's something wrong with its face."

"Let's call it Ugly," said a cheeky tadpole. "Old Ugly! There goes Old Ugly! Hi, Old Ugly! What's wrong with your face?"

The grub did not like being called names. It could not help being ugly. Nor could it help its enormous appetite. It was always hungry.

The water-snail sometimes crawled near to where Old Ugly lay in the mud. "Hallo, Old Ugly!" it would say. "Would you like me for your dinner? Well, you can't have me, because I can always pop back into my shell-house if you come too near. What's the matter with your face, Old Ugly?"

Certainly the grub had a curious face. The water-snail used to watch him, and see it change.

Sometimes the grub would lie quietly in the water – and then perhaps a cheeky tadpole would swim too near him.

At once a strange thing happened to his face. The lower part of it seemed to fall away – and out would shoot a kind of claw that caught hold of the tadpole. The claw put the little creature to the grub's mouth – and that was the end of him.

Then the grub would fold up this curious claw, and put it by his face, so that it seemed part of it. The water-snail was very curious about it.

"Show me how it works," he asked the grub. "No – I'm not coming too near you – and I'm only going to put my head out just a little, in case you think of taking hold of it. Now – show me how that funny claw-thing works."

The grub showed him. It was very clever the way he could fold it up below his face, so that it looked like part of it. It was on a hinge, and could be folded or unfolded just as he liked.

"It's a good idea," said the water-snail. "You are really rather a lazy creature, aren't you, Old Ugly – you like to lie about in the mud, and wait for your dinner to come to you. You don't like rushing about after it, like the water-beetle does. So that claw-thing is useful to you."

"Very useful," said the grub. "I can just lie here and wait – and then shoot out my claw – like this!"

The water-snail shot his head in just in time. "Don't play any tricks with *me*, Old Ugly," he said. "I tell you, I've got a hard shell. You could never eat me."

The other creatures in the pond were very careful not to go too near the grub. When they saw his face looking up out of the mud, they swam away quickly.

"That dreadful face!" said a gnat grub. "It is horrid the way it seems to fall to pieces when that lower part, the claw, shoots out. It really gives me a fright. There he is – look! Hallo, Old Ugly!"

"Don't call me that," said the grub. "It hurts me. I can't help being what I am. It is not my fault that I am ugly."

But nobody called him anything else. Nobody liked him. The snails teased him. The stickleback said that he would tear him to bits with his three spines if he went near his little nest of eggs. The tadpoles gathered round him at a safe distance and called him all the rude names they knew. And they knew a good many, for they were cheeky little things.

Even the frogs hated the grub. "He snapped at my leg today," said one. "I didn't see him in the mud down there, and I swam too near. Out shot that claw of his and gave my leg quite a nip."

"Let's turn him out of the pond," said the stickleback. "We don't want him here. He is ugly and greedy and fierce. If we all get together, we can turn him out."

So the stickleback, the frog, the two big black water-beetles, the tadpoles, the water-spider, the gnat grub, and the water-snails all swam or crawled to where Old Ugly was hiding in the mud, and called to him, "We don't want you in the pond!"

"Go away from here or I will tear you with my spines!"

"Leave our pond, or we will chase you round and round it till you are tired out!"

Old Ugly's face fell apart, and he shot out his long claw in anger. "How can I go away? There is nowhere for me to go to. I can't leave this pond. It is my home."

"You must leave it by to-morrow or we will bite you," said one of the water-beetles, the very fierce one.

"Yes, you must, or I shall rip you with my spines," said the stickleback, and he went scarlet with rage.

Well, of course, there was nowhere that the ugly grub could go. He could not breathe out of the water. He could not catch his dinner except in the pond.

He was sad and frightened. Next day the other creatures came to him again. The stickleback rushed at him and nearly pricked him with his spines. The fierce water-beetle tried to bite his tail.

"Go away!" cried the water-creatures. "Go away, Old Ugly."

Old Ugly felt ill. There was the stem of a water-plant near by and he began to crawl up it.

"Leave me alone," he said. "I feel ill."

The water-snail crawled after him. The stickleback tried to spear him with his spines.

The grub went on up the stem, and at last came to the top of the water. He crawled right out of the water, and stayed there on the stem, still feeling strange.

"Has he gone?" cried the tadpoles. "Has he gone?"

"He's out of the water," said the water-snail. Then he stared hard at the grub. "I don't think he feels very well," he said. "He looks a bit strange."

The grub stood still on the stem, and waited. He didn't know what he was waiting for, but he knew that something was going to happen. He felt very strange.

Then, quite suddenly, the skin began to split across his head. The water-snail saw it and called down to the creatures below:

"His skin has split! He really is ill! Something strange is happening to Old Ugly."

Something strange certainly *was* happening to the ugly grub. The skin split down his back too. Out from the top part came a head – a new head – a head with big brilliant eyes! The water-snail nearly fell from his leaf with astonishment.

"He's got a new head," he said. "And my goodness, he's got a new body too! His skin is splitting down his back. I can see his new body beneath."

"Is it as ugly as his old one?" asked a tadpole.

"No – it's beautiful – it's wonderful!" said the snail, watching patiently. And, indeed, it *was* wonderful. As time went on, the grub was able to wriggle completely out of his old skin.

He was no longer an ugly grub. He was a most beautiful dragonfly! His body gleamed bright green and blue – and what a long body it was! He had four wings, big, shining ones that quivered in the sun. He had wonderful eyes. He had six rather weak legs and a strong jaw.

"The ugly grub has changed into a dragonfly!" said the water-snail. "Oh, what a strange thing to see! Dragonfly, what has happened?"

"I don't know!" said the dragonfly, glad to feel his wings drying in the sun. "I don't know! I only know that for a long, long time I was an ugly grub in the pond – but that now I have wings, and I shall live in the air! Oh, what a wonderful time I shall have!"

When his wings were ready, the dragonfly darted high in the air on them, his blue and green body almost as bright as the kingfisher's feathers. He flew off, looking for insects to catch in his strong jaws. Snap – he caught a fly!

"What a beautiful creature!" said a little mouse in surprise, as the dragonfly whizzed past. "Hi, Beauty, Beauty, Beautiful! Where are you going?"

"Are you talking to *me*?" said the dragonfly in surprise. "I've always been called Old Ugly before!"

"You are lovely, lovely, *lovely*!" said the mouse. "Stay and talk to me, do!"

But the dragonfly was off again, darting through the air on strong wings, as happy as a swallow.

"What a strange life I have had!" he hummed to himself. "This is the nicest part. How happy I am, how happy I am!"

Maybe you will see him darting down the lane or over the pond. Look out for him, won't you, for he is one of the loveliest insects.

The Rabbit's Party

"I WANT to have a party," said Bobtail the rabbit. "It is my birthday very soon."

"I will help you with your party," said Big-Eyes the hare. "I will help you to write the cards to invite your friends to the party."

"Thank you," said Bobtail. "I shall ask Hoppy the frog. And Crawly the toad. And Flitter the bat."

"You must ask Dozy the dormouse," said Big-Eyes. "And you must not forget Scaly the snake. Do you want to ask Prickles the hedgehog?"

"Yes," said Bobtail. "But we must tell him not to sit close to anyone. He is not very nice to sit next to – we will give him a place by himself."

So they asked Hoppy the frog, Crawly the toad, Flitter the bat, Dozy the dormouse, Scaly the snake, and Prickles the hedgehog to come to the party.

They were all very excited. A party is such fun.

"Will there be some nice big flies to eat?" asked Hoppy the frog.

"Will you make me some beetle cake?" asked Prickles the hedgehog.

"Don't put me next to Scaly the snake, please," said Crawly the toad. "He might try to eat me for his tea. I shall make myself taste very nasty if he does, but it would spoil the party for me."

The party was to be on the last day of October. Bobtail did hope the weather would be fine. But in the last week of October the frost came and a cold wind blew. Bobtail shivered, and was glad that he had such a warm fur coat on.

"We had better not hold the party on the hillside," he said to Big-Eyes the hare. "It will be much too cold. We will hold it under the ground, down in my cosy burrow."

The day of the party came. Big-Eyes and Bobtail were very busy getting the tea ready. It was a fine tea. There were beetle cakes for Prickles and Flitter the bat. There were seed buns for Dozy the dormouse.

"Carrot cake for me, please," said Big-Eyes the hare. "Shall I go and catch some flies for Hoppy and Crawly to eat with their bread and butter, Bobtail?"

At three o'clock everything was ready. The rabbit and the hare waited for their friends to come.

But nobody came. Nobody at all.

"They are very late," said Bobtail, looking out of his burrow.

"There is no one on the hillside," said Big-Eyes. "Why are they so late? Have they forgotten?"

It was very sad. Nobody came to the party. Only Big-Eyes and Bobtail sat there, looking at the lovely tea.

"We must go and see why the others haven't come," said Bobtail at last. "Come along, Big-Eyes."

They ran out on to the hillside. They went to the pond, hoping to see Hoppy the frog. But he was not to be seen on the bank. They called him.

"Hoppy! Hoppy! Why don't you come to the party?"

The little robin called from a bush near by. "Hoppy is asleep! When the cold frost came at night he dived into the pond with the other frogs. He is in the mud at the bottom, fast asleep! Don't wake him. He will sleep all through the winter days."

"Dear me!" said Bobtail. "Well, *he* can't come to the party, then. Big-Eyes, we will fetch Crawly the toad."

They went to the big stone in the damp ditch, where Crawly often sat. They peeped underneath it. Crawly was there – but his eyes were shut.

"Crawly!" called Bobtail. "Why don't you come to the party?"

Crawly didn't wake up. He was fast asleep. The little robin sang loudly again to the rabbit and the hare.

"Crawly doesn't like the cold days and nights. He says there are no flies or grubs for him to eat. He has gone to sleep for the winter. Don't wake him."

"Bother!" said Big-Eyes. "*He* can't come to the party!"

"We will fetch Flitter the bat," said Bobtail. "He lives in that old barn over there."

So they went to the barn and peeped inside. It was dark and smelly. Bobtail looked up and saw many little black bats hanging up in the roof of the barn.

"They are all hanging upside down," he said to Big-Eyes in surprise. "How funny! They

have covered themselves with their wings. They must be asleep too."

"Yes, they are," said the robin, who had followed them. "Bats don't like the winter, you know. They always sleep soundly when it is very cold weather. Didn't you know that? Don't wake them."

"Oh dear!" said Bobtail. "Flitter can't come to the party. I can see him up there, fast asleep."

"What a pity!" said Big-Eyes. "Let's go and find Dozy the dormouse. He has a nice little home under the roots of a tree. I know where it is."

So they went to find Dozy. The robin flew beside them. The hole in the tree-roots was not big enough for Bobtail and Big-Eyes to go down. So they called Dozy.

"Dozy the dormouse! Come up at once. Have you forgotten it's the party?"

"Sh! Sh!" said the robin. "Dozy is asleep. He is afraid of the cold winter days, when the frost nips his tiny toes. He made himself nice and fat before he went to sleep. Don't wake him."

"Well, this is very sad," said Bobtail. "We will find Scaly the snake."

Scaly was in a hollow tree. Bobtail peeped in, but he could hardly see Scaly because the snake had curled himself up tightly with many other snakes like himself. There they were, all twisted up cosily together – fast asleep!

"Snakes always sleep in the winter-time," said the robin. "Don't wake Scaly. He won't like it."

"There's only Prickles the hedgehog left," said Bobtail sadly. "He lives in a hole in the bank over there."

So they went to Prickles' hole. He had lined it with dead leaves to make it cosy. There was a funny little noise coming from the hole.

"He's snoring," said the robin, flitting near. "He often does in the winter. He won't wake up whilst it is so cold. Don't wake him, will you? He's so snug down there."

Bobtail listened to the little snores that came from Prickles' hole. He looked very sad.

"I won't wake him," he said. "But, Robin, it is such a pity – Big-Eyes and I are having a party to-day, and not one of the friends we asked have come to it. They are all asleep."

"Well, you shouldn't have chosen people who would be asleep," said the robin.

"They were awake when we asked them," said Bobtail. "They said they would like to come to my birthday party."

"Oh, is it your birthday?" said the robin. "Many happy returns of the day."

"Thank you," said Bobtail. But he still looked sad.

"Ask Slinky the stoat," said the robin. "He is wide awake all the winter."

"No, thank you," said Bobtail at once. "He eats rabbits."

"Well, ask Wily the weasel," said the robin. "He stays awake all the winter, even when it's snowing."

"No, thank you," said Bobtail again. "He eats rabbits too."

"Well, what about Red-Coat the fox?" said

the robin. "He's always wide awake. He would love to come."

"You are being silly," said Bobtail. "Don't you know that foxes are always hunting rabbits? Think of something sensible."

The robin thought hard. "You could ask *me*," he said at last. "I don't eat rabbits. But I should very much like beetle-cake, or bread-and-butter and flies."

"Well, you come, then," said Bobtail, cheering up. "It's funny that so many animals like to sleep in the winter. It's quite a good idea, really, if you don't like the cold and you can't get food to eat. But it has spoilt my party."

It didn't spoil it after all, because the robin brought a sparrow, a thrush, and two jolly blackbirds to the party. They ate all the food, they sang songs, and they played "Catch a feather from my tail", which was great fun.

"Well, it was a lovely party," said Bobtail happily, hopp ing into his burrow after he had said goodbye to his guests. "I'm very tired and sleepy now. But *I* shan't sleep all the winter away! Oh no – I shall wake up tomorrow."

And, of course, he did.

The Dog That Remembered

PETER was such a lucky boy. Nice things were always happening to him.

"My uncle is taking me to the circus!" he would say to the other children. Or, "My Auntie is giving me a tricycle! Think of that!"

When he was ill his Granny took him his favourite jellies. They were nice jellies, the top half pink and the lower half yellow. His Grandpa sent him a fine jigsaw puzzle that made a wonderful steamer when it was all fitted together.

Once when he fell into the river a bigger boy jumped in and saved him. The big boy got his clothes wet and spoilt his new tie, but he didn't make a fuss about that. He was glad to have saved Peter.

But Peter never seemed grateful for anything, and sometimes he didn't even remember to say thank you. His mother used to worry about this.

"You are such a lucky little boy, Peter," she said. "You have so many nice things given to you, and so many lovely treats. People are so kind to you when you are ill – and if you are in trouble they always help you. But you never seem to remember their kindness."

"Don't I?" said Peter, in surprise. "How ought I to remember their kindness then?"

"Well, Granny was good to you when you were ill, and you should go and see her more often, and take her some flowers from your garden," said his mother. "And that boy who dived in and saved you from the river – you never even went to see if his clothes had dried all right. You didn't even offer to buy him a new tie when you knew his own had been quite spoilt. And you had plenty of money in your money-box."

"Oh," said Peter. "I didn't think."

"Well, you ought to think," said his mother. "I keep thinking for you, but it's not the same thing."

Now one day when Peter was out in the woods, he heard a dog whining in pain. He looked about and soon found a little puppy whose foot had been caught in a rabbit-trap.

"Poor thing!" said Peter. "I'll set you free –and I'll throw the trap away so that it can never catch and hurt any animal so cruelly again!"

He knew how to open the trap. Soon the dog was free. It licked its paw, still whining. It licked Peter's hand too, and looked up at him out of grateful brown eyes.

"Poor fellow!" said Peter, patting him. "I'm glad I came along. Go home, and get your foot seen to."

The dog went off, limping on three legs, holding its hurt paw up in the air. It still whined, for it was in pain.

The next day the dog appeared outside Peter's home. Its hurt foot was neatly bound up, and Peter was glad. He looked at the dog and the dog looked at him.

"Woof," said the dog, and licked Peter's hand.

"He has come to say thank you," said Peter's mother. "Isn't that good of him?"

The dog trotted away again. It was back the next day, and this time it brought a big bone in its mouth. It waited till Peter came out, and then it ran to him and laid the bone at his feet.

"Oh Mother, look! The dog has brought me its bone!" cried Peter. "Dear old dog – I don't want your bone, but thank you for bringing it!"

A week later Peter was running through the

woods when a tramp stepped out from some bushes. "Hi, wait!" said the tramp. "Have you any money? If you have, you must give it to me!"

Peter was frightened. He had two ten pence pieces and he didn't want to give them to this rough man. He tried to slip away but the tramp caught him.

"Now then!" he said, and gave Peter a slap on the cheek. "Don't you try to run away! You give me your money!"

"Help! Help!" cried Peter, trying to get away. But there was no one in the woods that day. The tramp shook the boy hard, and Peter almost fell over.

Then, through the woods there came the pattering of feet, and the dog ran up. He still ran on three paws, for the fourth one hurt him.

He leapt at the tramp with a fierce growl. The man let go of Peter at once and put up his hands to defend himself.

"Call him off, call him off!" he said. "Don't let him bite me!"

But the dog nipped him well at the back of the leg, and the tramp fled through the woods, howling. Peter sat down, trembling. The dog sat close by him, licking him every now and

again, looking up at him out of big brown eyes.

"Woof," he said. Peter put his arm round him. "You are a wonderful dog," he said. "All I did was to set you free from a trap, and you have never forgotten. You came and thanked me. You gave me a present of a bone you must have badly wanted to eat yourself – and now you have saved me from being robbed by that horrid tramp."

"Woof," said the dog, and licked him again.

"Come home with me and let me tell Mother

what you have done," said Peter. So they went home, and Peter told his mother the whole story.

"Isn't he a wonderful dog?" said Peter. His mother nodded.

"Yes," she said. "He is better than a little boy I know! He is grateful – he says thank you – he brings a little present – and he waits for a chance to show how grateful he is, by saving you from that tramp!"

"How funny that a dog should be better than I am!" said Peter, going rather red. "He keeps on and on remembering the kindness I did to him, doesn't he, Mother? He doesn't forget, like I do. Well, I love him for remembering, and I shall always be friends with him!"

And now Peter too remembers to be grateful when people are kind to him. He is great friends with the dog, and they go for long walks together – but wasn't it funny that a dog had to teach him never to forget a kindness?

Mooo-ooo-ooo!

ONCE upon a time there was a little girl called Lucy. She lived in a big town, and every year she went to the seaside.

But one year she went to stay in the country instead. Her mother sent her to stay with her Aunt Mary on a big farm.

"You will have such a lovely time, Lucy," said her mother. "You will have chickens and ducks round you, big sheep in the fields, and perhaps Aunt Mary will let you ride on one of the big horses."

"Will there be cows?" asked Lucy.

"Oh yes," said her mother. "Lovely big red and white cows that say 'Mooo-ooo-ooo!' You will like them, Lucy."

"I shan't," said Lucy. "I'm afraid of cows."

"Silly girl," said her mother. "There's no need to be afraid of cows. They won't hurt you."

"They might toss me with their big horns," said Lucy.

"Of course they won't," said her mother. "Cows are gentle animals. You will like them."

But Lucy didn't like them. As soon as she was down at the farm, she began to look out for cows. She saw some in a field – and oh dear, as she walked by the field, one of the cows put its head over the hedge and mooed loudly.

"Mooo-ooo-ooo!" it said. It did make poor Lucy jump. She ran home crying, and her aunt was sorry.

"Darling, the cows won't hurt you," she said. "They are our friends. They give us lots of nice things, really they do."

"They don't give *me* anything," sobbed Lucy. "At least, they only give me nasty things. That cow gave me a horrid fright."

"Well, come with me and feed the hens," said Aunt Mary. Lucy dried her eyes and went with her aunt.

When she came back again it was eleven o'clock. Her aunt went to the larder and brought out a bun. Then she poured some rich yellow milk into a blue cup.

"A present from the cow," she said to Lucy. "Drink it up and see how nice it is. The cow gave it to me this morning, and I put it in a jug for you."

Lucy tasted the milk. It was simply lovely. "It's much nicer than my milk at home," she said. "Did the cow really give it to me?"

"Yes, it came from the cow," said Aunt Mary. "As soon as you stop being afraid of my dear old cows, I want you to come with me and see me milk them. You will like to hear the milk splashing into the pail. It is a lovely sound."

When dinner-time came, there was an apple pie for pudding. Lucy was glad.

"It's one of my favourite puddings," she said. "Is there any custard, Auntie?"

"No," said her aunt. "But the cow sent you this instead. You will like it."

Aunt Mary put a little blue jug of cream down beside Lucy's plate. "Pour it out over your pie yourself," she said. "It is all for you. Have it all and enjoy it. Isn't the cow kind?"

Lucy poured out the cream over her pie. It was thick and yellow and tasted very good.

In the afternoon she went out to play, but she didn't go near the field where the cows were. "If I do they will shout 'Mooo-ooo-ooo' at me again," she said to herself.

When tea-time came Lucy was hungry. She was glad to hear the tea-bell and ran indoors. There was a loaf of crusty new bread on the table, and beside it was a white dish full of golden-yellow butter. There was a pot of strawberry jam, and some buns. Lucy thought it was a lovely tea.

"What lovely golden butter!" she said. "Can I spread it on my piece of bread myself, Auntie? Mother lets me at home."

"Yes, you can," said Aunt Mary. "It's a present from the cow again."

"*Is* it?" said Lucy, surprised. "I didn't know butter came from the cow."

"Well, we make it from the cream that we get from the milk that the cow gives us," said Aunt Mary. "So it is really a present from the cow, too, you see."

"Oh," said Lucy, spreading her bread with the rich yellow butter. "The cow *does* give us a lot of things, doesn't it?"

Lucy met the cows that evening as they walked to their milking-place. One mooed rather loudly and she ran away again. She told her aunt about it at supper-time.

"That nasty horrid cow mooed loudly at me again," she said. "I don't like cows. They are horrid things."

"Dear me, I'm sorry," said Aunt Mary, as she set down Lucy's supper in front of her. "I suppose you won't want to eat another present from the cow, then?"

"Does this lovely cheese come from the cow too?" cried Lucy, in great surprise. "Oh, Aunt Mary – I didn't know that! Milk – and cream –and butter – and cheese! Well, really, what a nice animal!"

Lucy ate her bread and butter and cheese. She had some stewed apple and cream, and she drank a glass of milk. What a number of things came from the cow! She thought about it quite a lot.

"Auntie," she said the next day, "I think I am wrong to be silly about cows. But I can't help it. Do you think if I got used to baby cows first, I would grow to like grown-up cows?"

"I am sure you would," said Aunt Mary. "That is a very good idea! We have some calves, and you shall help me to feed them today. You shall see me feed a little new-born calf. You will like that."

"Do calves grow into cows?" asked Lucy, trotting after her aunt.

"Oh yes, always," said Aunt Mary. "Now look, here is our very youngest baby. We must teach her to suck milk. We cannot let her suck her mother's milk – that big cow over there –because we want all *her* milk to sell; so we must feed her out of a pail."

The baby calf was very sweet. She was rather wobbly on her long legs, and she had the softest brown eyes that Lucy had ever seen. She sniffed at Lucy's hand and then began to suck it.

"Oh – she's very hungry, Auntie," said Lucy. "She's trying to suck my hand."

It wasn't long before Aunt Mary had a pail of milk ready for the calf. "Now watch me teach her to drink," she said.

She dipped her fingers in the milk and held them out to the calf. The calf sniffed the milk and then licked it eagerly, trying to take Aunt Mary's hand into her mouth. She dipped her fingers in the pail of milk again, and once more the calf licked the milk off.

The next time Aunt Mary did not hold her fingers out so far. She held them in the pail. The calf put her head in the pail, and followed her fingers down. Aunt Mary put them right into the milk as soon as the calf began to suck them.

Then the little creature found that she was sucking up a great deal of milk! She still nuzzled around Aunt Mary's fingers, but she couldn't help taking in some of the milk in the pail, for her mouth was in it!

"That's a clever way of teaching her to drink milk," said Lucy, delighted. "Let me put *my* fingers in, Aunt Mary. I want to do it too."

So Aunt Mary held the pail whilst Lucy dipped her fingers in, and let the calf suck them. Then slowly the little girl put them nearer to the milk, until once again the calf was drinking in the pail!

"She will soon learn," said Aunt Mary. "You can help me to feed the little thing three times a day, if you like, dear."

So for the next week or two Lucy helped to feed the little calf. She loved her, and then one day she found that she was no longer afraid of cows!

"I can't be afraid of you when I love your little calf so much," she told the big red and white cow. "The little calf will grow up to be just like you, and she will give me presents like you do – milk and cream and butter and cheese. Thank you, cow. I'm sorry I ever said you were horrid. I like you now, big red cow, and one day I'll help to milk you!"

"Moo-ooo-ooo!" said the cow, pleased. "Moo-ooo-oooo!"

The Rich Little Dog

THERE was once a little dog called Prince. He belonged to a rich mistress, who made a great pet of him. Prince had a bowl with his name on. He had a beautiful basket lined with warm blankets. He had three collars and a really beautiful lead.

He thought himself very grand indeed and when he went out walking he hardly looked at the other dogs. He put his nose in the air and walked along slowly, his tail up, his ears cocked, and every hair in its place. He was brushed and combed each day and if his mistress could have made him clean his teeth she would.

"Here comes old High-and-Mighty!" sniffed Bimbo when he saw Prince coming.

"He's got a coat on today!" wuffed Spot, in surprise. "Hi, you! Why do you wear a coat?"

"To keep me warm, of course," said Prince. "How stupid you are!"

"I keep warm all right without a coat!" said Rough, barking round Prince in a most annoying manner. "I just run around and I'm as warm as toast."

"Don't bark at my heels like that," said Prince. "And don't splash near me in puddles. You will spoil my new red coat with muddy drops."

Rough splashed him all over. Prince was very angry, but the other dogs only laughed at him.

"Now, now!" wuffed Prince, annoyed. "You can't do that sort of thing to me! I'm a very well-brought-up dog, I am. I've a bowl with my name on and a basket lined with a red blanket. I've got three collars, each with my name and address on. I'm very, very valuable."

"Yes, you may be, but you're as dull as ditch-water!" barked Bimbo. "I haven't a bowl with my name on, but I have a good hard bone each day to gnaw, which *you* never get!"

"And I haven't a red coat to wear, but I can always lie inside the fender at home, and *you* can't!" wuffed Rough.

"And I know where hundreds of rabbits live and all *you* know is the smell of the rubbish-heap at the bottom of the next-door garden!" yelped Spot.

Prince went home feeling cross. How dare these common little dogs pretend that their life was better than his. He was a prince among dogs, very valuable, petted and fussed all day long. He trotted to his mistress, expecting to be petted. He jumped on to her lap.

But she put him down at once. "Prince! What have you done to your beautiful red coat? It's all spotted with mud. Really, it's very naughty of you. Now I shall have to brush it well."

Next morning it was very cold again. Prince's mistress buttoned his coat round him and told him to go and have a run, and then come straight back in case he got a cold that bleak and frosty day. So out trotted Prince most obediently, determined not to get his beautiful red coat dirty again.

All the other dogs – Bimbo, Rough, Spot, Lucky, Tim, Topsy and Bobs – were gathered together excitedly in a corner. Spot was wuffing loudly.

"It's just a day to go rabbiting. It's so cold. It will be fun to tear up the hill and go chasing those rabbits that live there. They pop in and out of holes, you know, and it's lovely to watch for them, and chase them, and try to dig them out. What about it, friends?"

There was a loud barking from everyone. It

all sounded most exciting. Prince trotted up. "Could I come and watch?" he wuffed.

"You'd get your coat dirty, old High-and-Mighty," said Bimbo.

"You might lose your collar," said Spot.

"You'd ruffle your hair," said Rough.

"You'd come back without your stuck-up tail," said Topsy.

"You'd get puffed, you'd lose your way, and all the rabbits would chase you when they saw you!" said Lucky, rudely.

The dogs set off down the road, turned up a lane, and tore up the hill. Prince couldn't bear to be left behind. He found himself tearing after them, too, puffing loudly because he hadn't run fast for a long time. The rabbits were out on the hillside. With excited barks the dogs chased them here, there and everywhere. Prince watched round-eyed as he saw the rabbits popping in and out of holes like magic. They smelt exciting. They looked exciting.

And quite suddenly Prince wanted to chase them, too. So he joined in. He barked loudly. He missed his footing and rolled halfway down the hill, tearing his red coat. He caught his collar on a gorse-bush, and in trying to get it free, it came off, and he left it behind.

A rabbit sprang near him and he jumped at it. He missed it and landed in a patch of mud. His red coat began to look brown. He tore after the rabbit, which went into a hole.

Prince began to scrape hard at the hole. He *must* make it big enough to get down, he must, he must, he must. His eyes were full of dirt, his ears were full of dirt, his coat was full of dirt. But Prince didn't care. He was hot, dirty, without a collar, and with a very torn red coat – but he didn't care! He wasn't a valuable pet dog any more, he was just an ordinary fellow, mad to get at a rabbit. And he was very happy.

Nobody caught a rabbit. They never did. It wasn't the rabbits that mattered, it was really the hunting about after them that was so exciting. The dogs pattered down the hillside, tired, but happy.

"I say, look at Prince!" said Rough, suddenly. "I didn't know him. Whatever will your mistress say to you, Prince?"

"Don't know and don't care," said Prince. "I wasn't a dog before. I was just a silly pet. Now I'm a dog. And I'm going to *stay* one."

He went home. His mistress rose from her chair in horror when she saw him. "PRINCE!" What *have* you been doing? You bad, wicked dog! You've lost that nice collar. You've torn your beautiful coat! You're dirty and smelly. I don't like you at all. You can go outside to the kennel and stay there till you're sorry."

Prince went out into the kennel. The straw smelt good. He lapped up some water, then lay down and fell alseep, dreaming of rabbits. He was very happy.

The other dogs don't laugh at him any more. He won't wear his red coat, and he won't use his lined basket. His mistress is disappointed in him, and doesn't like him. But the little boy next door loves him, and so do all the dogs in the town.

"You're a *real* prince now!" they wuff, when he leads them off on a rabbit-hunt. "One day you may even catch a rabbit!"

He may, of course – but he hasn't yet!